PAYING FOR
PAIN

PAYING FOR
PAIN

Paul McGoran

NEW PULP PRESS

Published by New Pulp Press, LLC, 926 Truman Avenue, Key West, Florida 33040, USA.

For information contact:
Publisher@NewPulpPress.com

ISBN-13: 978-0692594742 (New Pulp Press)
ISBN-10: 0692594744

"Ask me who the devil is, I'll tell ya. The devil is every stinkin' surprise that comes along to tweak your tits and grind you in the dirt."

- Paying for Pain

PAYING FOR
PAIN

INTRODUCTION

What Is Noir, Anyway?

Crime fiction comes in lots of flavors. Among others, you'll encounter varieties like 'cozy,' 'police procedural,' 'hardboiled,' and 'noir.' Each of these sub-genres adheres to certain conventions in the presentation of character and subject matter. What follows is a short gloss on the 'noir' tradition, including my personal interpretation of this small, but influential slice of the mystery/thriller universe.

With the rise of crime as a popular subject for fiction in the nineteenth century, it was natural that the crime solver, whether police detective or private investigator, came to fill the role of protagonist in stories dedicated to criminal subject matter. The private detective, in particular, proved to be a godsend for writers looking to establish a novel series. In the twentieth century, noir fiction began as an offshoot of the hardboiled detective story, wherein a tough-talking private eye staggers through the urban crudscape with few ideals apart from his sense of honor and a rough standard of justice.

You'll recognize 'noir' as a French word meaning black. By extension, it has connotations of darkness, bleakness – even hopelessness. As a branch of crime fiction, noir has the edgy attitude of hardboiled, but usually exchanges the gritty private eye stereotype for a sweaty-faced everyman, an average Joe or Jane under pressure. By anticipating a story's outcome, we can highlight the boundary between the two genres: a P.I. will surely prove his or her mettle, but in noir we remain in suspense about the lead character. He may triumph, collapse under pressure, or wind up in jail for someone else's crimes. The possibility of failure accounts for the frequency of the standalone novel in noir.

Crime fiction writer Jack Bludis gives us a handy summary of the distinction between protagonists in the two genres when he says, "Hardboiled = tough, noir = screwed."

In America, the establishing authors of noir were James M. Cain and Cornell Woolrich. Other early exponents who come to mind are Horace McCoy, Jim Thompson, Patricia Highsmith and Charles Williams. Donald Westlake and Elmore Leonard continued their storied careers until their deaths in the twenty-first century. Masters still in the game are James Ellroy, Max Allan Collins and Lawrence Block.

As a literary term in English, 'noir' is a retrofit. French publishers used the label '*série noir*' to distinguish more generalized crime fiction from the '*policier*' – detective fiction featuring police work. '*Film noir*' is a phrase first used by French critics in the 1950's to describe the fatalistic black and white crime films of 1940's Hollywood which, in their turn, were often adapted from hardboiled or noir originals – then known simply as detective stories or crime stories.

With that thumbnail sketch of its origins in mind, let's consider the building blocks of noir. In my definition, there are five essentials. To begin with, there must be a **CRIME**. Most times it's murder, but a heist will do. Even an adulterous relationship might serve, especially if it leads to a scenario of anxiety-filled flight and pursuit.

Arguably more important than the crime in noir is the **OBSESSION**. Often the two will be related. The obsession may be a sculpture of a falcon with a long and fatal history, or the mysterious substance hidden by a secret cabal in the wine cellar. In more recent productions, it tends toward drugs, fame, power, or wealth. It might even be obsession itself if the writer affects an intellectual bent. Most often, it is simply the McGuffin, Hitchcock's term for the elusive, essentially meaningless, prop that sets the plot in motion. Typically, this device serves to elicit reactions from the story's characters in ways that reveal the varieties of human deceit and corruption.

FATALISM in noir fiction is more pervasive attitude than absolute certainty. The noir protagonist – flawed and confused, but determined – knows in his soul the sense of impending doom he struggles against can only be overcome with the greatest possible effort. He may win or lose, but even a victory is likely to come at great cost. His crime, his difficulty, has terrible consequences, and they almost always involve death – whether his or someone else's.

From mental states to sexual desire, **PERVERSITY** is another key notion in the noir canon. All kinds of novels and films haul in kinky sex nowadays, but noir sex almost always includes the element of *amour fou* – mad, obsessive desire – the brand of love that hurts. Perversity isn't just about sex, however. It's also about contrariness and inversion, a habit of looking at life differently from everybody else, especially the authority figures that write the laws and compile the rulebooks.

A final item you can count on in noir is **BETRAYAL**, which lurks in each dark street and every plot twist. In classic noir, the lead character is a man under extreme pressure, and the ultimate betrayal comes with the unexpectedness of a random, savage knife thrust – from the woman he trusted, often against his own better judgment. Whether the betrayer is a femme fatale or an homme fatal is irrelevant in today's world, but the betrayal itself is an absolute noir necessity.

To my mind, that's noir in a nutshell, a potent brew of transgression and dark psychology that takes crime and its consequences seriously, even while it provides emotional catharsis and a few fervid thrills along the way for its aficionados. Long may it live!

The Geography of Noir

In the present collection of dark stories, emphasis lies on the *geography* of noir. Location in noir is traditionally, but not exclusively, urban. Rain-slicked streets, tall buildings, and shadowy doorways are embedded in our consciousness from a host of classic movies. They often serve as triggers to establish the noir milieu. Still, noir can take place nearly anywhere. Well, maybe not so much at Disney World or at restaurants serving Happy Meals. Substitute a cheesy carnival or a roadside diner, however, and we're back in business.

Two venues for noir will be conspicuous by their absence in *Paying for Pain*. I've left out the great urban instruments that Chandler and Woolrich fingered and bowed with such virtuosity – Los Angeles and New York. After all, who in hell could improve on their achievements?

I believe it's fair to say that geography is one determinant for temperature. And there's no doubt heat is an atmospheric conductor for noir. That's why settings like Mexico, south Florida, and Vegas were chosen for *Paying for Pain*. Symbolically, a rising thermometer serves to point up a character's anxiety as well as put sweat on his face. Crime, heat, lust, rage and dread – they simply go together, right?

That's not to say the cooler regions of San Francisco and the Northeast don't work for noir. These are classic urban playgrounds where crowded neighborhoods and a strong sense of the past have conspired to invest this collection of stories with some of its most jaded and desperate characters.

So turn the page, pick a town, and take a darkside vacation. Or settle in for a bumpy night with the whole twisted travelogue that lies ahead. After all, I prepared it especially for you.

THE STORIES:

The Thanks You Get
Vegas Noir – A hard guy in Las Vegas looks to his sidekick for help when the going gets tough, then shows his appreciation. **Page 7**

Beach of the Dead
Tropical Trackdown Noir – When Vinny Guyett absconds to Mexico with the union's healthcare premiums, Irvin Palazzo assigns a crew to murder him and retrieve the money. Never give the finger to a killer. **Page 17**

Paying for Pain
Northeast Urban Noir – Our boy Harold interviews assassins for a little project he has in mind. In the end, he realizes it's family that matters. **Page 41**

Summer of Porkpie
Noir Suspense in Two Towns – Three characters narrate their involvement with Samson Porter, a.k.a. Porkpie. Spend the summer with them – first in trendy South Beach with Kristi Darnell, then in elegant Newport with Ivan Chitworth and Helena Swann. **Page 53**

No Good Deed (a novella)
Mission District Noir – Mickey Cullion is a little ex-con who runs a storefront church in San Francisco called The Breastplate of Faith and Love. But his efforts at redemption falter when a long-kept secret is revealed, prompting a fresh round of blackmail ... and murder. No good deed goes unpunished at the Breastplate of Faith and Love. **Page 79**

THE THANKS YOU GET

Henry Shevlin didn't like Las Vegas much and he didn't like the way his life was going. But he was the type to do anything for a friend. It was Duke Santoro who liked the town. Off and on, Henry had been living with Duke for three years and had known him a couple years more in stir.

They shared a room in a rundown courtyard motel at the north end of the Strip where it turns kind of sleazy. The bed was near the window overlooking the cars in the courtyard. Henry was lying there in his skivvies reading a magazine when he saw Duke out of the corner of his eye. He was snaking through the rows of parked cars, taking a diagonal route toward the stairs to the second floor balcony that the rooms gave out on. He had the easy long stride of an athlete, really a pleasure to watch. In a minute he pushed open the door to the room.

Right away, Henry could tell Duke was agitated. He walked in real quiet, took off his jacket and draped it over the desk chair. Then he turned, walked to the right side of the bed and sat on it. After loosening his tie, he shook out a cigarette from a pack on the bedside table and fired it with a kitchen match. All this without a word.

Henry figured what the hell, get it out in the open. "Hey, big fella, what's up?"

"Nothing."

"Can't be nothing, Duke. You're pissed off. Anybody can tell."

"It's that little bitch, Lana. She didn't show up tonight."

"She, uh, told you she would?"

"No, but she always does on Tuesday. She's stepping

7

out with that kid Randy she talks about."

"Hell, that's just to make you jealous is all. She's crazy about you."

"I don't like anybody cutting in on me. I can't take it and I won't."

He got up then, still smoking, and paced the floor. Henry watched him for a minute before saying: "Just let it go, Duke. Show her you don't fall for that routine."

"You know I won't put up with it, Henry."

"That's right, big guy, you don't have to. Just ignore her. She'll come calling."

"Shit!"

If Duke seemed agitated before, he was at the boiling point now. His lip curved up in a sneer and his nostrils flared. He stubbed his cigarette out, stopped pacing and stripped to the waist. Then he sat on the bed, his back to Henry.

He knew he'd best shut up and wait, so he tossed the magazine to the floor and shifted down in bed, lying there with his head propped up to keep an eye on Duke. When he was sure the storm had passed, he turned to switch off the bedside lamp.

~ ~ ~

Next morning, he was in the parking lot, reading the paper and waiting for Duke to come down. He always took longer than Henry to get ready. Duke would shave and shower, same as him, but he put a lot extra into it. He was especially fussy about the way he dressed. Neither of them had a lot of clothes, but Duke sure knew how to vary his look and keep his duds looking fresh.

Henry saw him step out to the landing from the room and look up to the clear, bright sky. He headed down the outside stairs to the parking area. That quick stride of his brought him over to the car in no time. He was dressed in a dark sport jacket, tan slacks and an open collar shirt.

Henry pushed himself off the side of the car and folded his newspaper.

"I have to be at the bar by nine for my shift, Duke."

"Okay," he said. "Me, I'm gonna take the day off. Want to go to breakfast?"

"Yeah, well I do, but I'm nearly broke. I was figuring on maybe a coffee and donut."

"Hell no, dude, I'm flush! Tell you what, I'll spring for the whole megillah."

Henry pointed to the car and smiled. "Lead the way, my man! What are you going to tell your boss?"

"Haven't decided. But I picked up eight hundred bucks shooting dice last night and I'm not gonna be dealing no cards for a couple of days."

"Say, Duke, you almost never gamble."

"Never for long, anyway. The percentages are lousy."

They drove to a diner type restaurant just beyond Fremont Street and were eating breakfast in a booth by the front window when Lana Firewood walked in. She had a slim young dark-haired guy with her who was grinning from ear to ear. Henry saw her glance around and then turn to speak to Smiley. He figured she must have spotted them and he kind of held his breath for what would happen next. Duke hadn't seen a thing yet.

Lana walked straight towards them, high heels clattering across the tiles, her boyfriend trailing behind like a happy puppy. As they came close, Henry looked up. She gave him a little wave while she still had Duke's back to her. Finally, she made a point of stopping and turning around when she passed them by.

"Oh hi, Duke!" she said, acting all surprised. "I didn't recognize you from behind."

Duke looked from one to the other, still chewing on a piece of toast. He nodded real quick and grunted. This may have been rude, but Henry was glad he didn't speak because it sure as hell would have been ruder. Lana looked annoyed, squaring her shoulders and biting her lower lip.

"Good to see you, Henry," she said, turning and walking past with Smiley to an empty booth further down the aisle.

Duke put down his knife and fork, took the napkin out of his lap and tossed it on the table. His face was flushed.

"Come on," said Henry, "don't let her get to you. You know what she's doing."

"When I was a bouncer, I occasionally took a certain amount of pleasure in leaning on somebody who insisted on getting out of line. Pain is a terrific agent for rapid attitude change."

"She's trying to make you jealous. So forget it. Screw her!"

"Screwing her is apparently one of the easiest and cheapest things to do in Las Vegas. Like being comped for a buffet lunch. I think both of them need a rapid attitude change."

"C'mon man, take it easy."

Henry was getting nervous and Duke had to see it. But he took a deep breath and seemed to calm down.

"Listen, no rush Hank," he said, "but as soon as you're done here, I'll drop you off at work. I'm gonna take a long ride."

When Henry asked him where to, Duke didn't answer. His face was set tight and he stared straight ahead with a kind of dark expression that Henry couldn't even begin to describe.

~ ~ ~

Duke watched as Randy and Lana pulled up to her house in the valley around ten o'clock. They weren't aware of anyone following, he was sure. As he passed them, he saw her slide up close to Randy at the wheel for a long, wet kiss.

Jesus, he was ready to do them right there and then, whoever might see it be damned. There were red spots in his vision and his breath was coming fast, but he shook it off. So he could do it right, he said to himself.

He knew what was going on because Lana had brought him there just last week. She had given him the same kind of wet, lingering kiss she favored Randy with today. He even remembered their conversation in front of the house.

"You know, nobody's home right now and I could sure use some company," she had said.

"Use me baby, I'm your boy!" Duke laughed.

"O-o-o-o, it's a boy!" she squealed, moving her hand into his crotch.

Both of them were laughing by then. They rushed out of the car, met at the curb and ran to the front door holding hands.

Today, he parked on the new service road behind Lana's house at the edge of the subdivision. A wooded ravine separated her neighborhood from the road. No way they could see his car from her place. He doubled back, climbing through the ravine and brush behind the house. As he approached, he could hear Lana's dog barking.

It didn't take long for him to get into the garage and quietly jimmy the door to the kitchen. It was cool inside and a little dark. After hesitating a moment, he walked to the kitchen island and sat on a stool, where he waited patiently.

Lana and Randy had come into the living room through the front door. Duke heard her making baby noises to the dog and laughing with Randy. The television came on loud, nearly drowning out their conversation.

"The kitchen's right through there, Randy," she said. "Why don't you get us a couple beers?"

As he pushed through the swinging door, Randy looked around for the refrigerator. But his eyes locked on

Duke, still sitting quietly on the stool by the kitchen island.

"Get out, son," he said in low, even voice. "Just leave."

"Who the hell let you in?" asked Randy.

"It's real simple. I belong here, Junior. You don't."

"Really? Well, it's not like we're in competition, pal. Lana's been around the block. But I'm here now and intend to get what I came for."

When Duke stood and moved toward him, Randy pulled a knife. The boy was nothing if not game. Duke grabbed his blade arm and stripped the knife away with his other hand. In close quarters, Randy tried to bring his knee up, but the big guy pivoted slightly and launched a right uppercut.

As he went down, Randy's arm cleared the kitchen counter. While sprawled out on the floor, he reached for the wooden knife block that had tumbled down with him. Deftly, he withdrew a meat cleaver and rose to attack.

The first blow struck home and Duke sustained a wicked defensive cut across the back of his left hand. But he sidestepped the second strike, pulled the cleaver out of Randy's grip and knocked him down again with a right hand blow that crunched into his face and broke his nose. Blood and snot gushed out and Randy was moaning, beaten. Duke felt his own blood rise inside him as never before.

"A cleaver, you fucking idiot!" he exploded. "I don't believe you went after me with a cleaver."

Poor Randy had to see it coming from the way Duke looked at him. The big man hefted the cleaver and hacked at him from the throat down, pausing only to kick his head in when Randy feebly raised his hands to make him stop.

Lana must have heard the racket, even though it was muffled by the blare from the television.

"Randy!" she yelled. "What's going on in there?"

Her mutt was yapping now in that hysterical tone

small dogs have. Duke scrambled out of sight to the side of the refrigerator. He was covered in sweat and his hair hung down on his forehead. He saw Lana come through the door with the pooch trailing. She looked at Randy on the floor and all that blood, made a choking sound, and wobbled backwards. When she turned and spotted Duke, her eyes registered confusion, then relief – as if she were glad to see someone who could help. He moved to her quickly, spun her around and snapped her neck before she could utter more than a quiet whimper.

He needed a minute to calm down. When his heart stopped pounding, he tried to think logically. Lucky for him, he didn't have a whole lot of blood on his clothes. He washed up, found a dishtowel to stanch the cut on his hand, then wiped down every surface he had touched. Before leaving, he coaxed the quivering dog into the living room, took a careful look around the kitchen and pocketed Randy's knife. A minute later he was back in his car on the service road.

~ ~ ~

Henry was at the motel when Duke came back that day at two in the afternoon. It was sure easy to tell something was up. He was chain smoking and looked glassy-eyed. There was gauze wrapped around his left hand with some white tape over that.

At first Henry didn't see the stains, but the big man's clothes were all wrinkled and there was a bulge in his jacket pocket that turned out to be a little towel with blood on it. When Duke whipped that sucker out, it seemed to trigger something. He laughed, sat on the bed and talked about what happened at Lana's house.

Henry couldn't believe it at first; Duke was saying some scary stuff, over and over. When it all came clear, he figured the best he could do was not act upset, but be calm, help him out.

"You totally lost it, Duke," he said. "But you gotta get yourself together fast. Take it easy now, real easy. We have to stay cool. Okay, pal?"

"Okay, Henry. I get it," he said.

They both knew the clothes had to go. Henry had him strip absolutely everything off so he could take care of getting it incinerated. Shoes and socks, and the towel too. All of a sudden, he was into it, helping his friend, telling him what to do. Did he think Duke would be grateful, or like him better? Probably that was it.

And he did a damn fine job. He unwound the makeshift bandage and saw that Duke needed stitches. Now this was a little tricky, but biting the bullet and going to an emergency room with the right story should take care of it.

"You got all that dough from gambling last night, Duke, so what the hell. Give them a phony name, tell them you was chopping up a chicken with a butcher knife, and get a few stitches."

"Yeah. That sounds about right."

"Other than that, get cleaned up and get out of town."

Henry figured he would stay in Vegas, go to work like usual. Nobody had anything on him; that part he didn't have to worry about. The motel room was in his name alone, nobody could link him with Duke too much, he was just a buddy who came and went. They hadn't been here so long that a lot of people knew them.

Duke made a bundle of his bloody clothes and shoes, wrapping it all up with his jacket and tying the arms together. Henry knew just where to go when it got dark. There was an alley not far away where a few alkies would be warming themselves over a fire barrel. Even Las Vegas gets cool in January.

Piece by piece in the darkness, the clothes flared up and disappeared. An old greybeard wino laughed like hell every time Henry popped another article of clothing into the barrel. The shoes went in last, and somehow that made the old man mad. The poor bastard probably saw they were better than the half-rotted sneakers he had on.

When Henry walked back to the motel, he had that nice feeling you get from putting things in order. As they agreed beforehand, he rapped softly on the door four times and waited. Duke opened it and pulled him in, that thousand-yard stare of his telling Henry everything had changed. Still, the little guy got his shiv out fast, like a magician pulling a dove out of his coat. Not that it mattered too much with Duke grabbing his wrist and spinning him around, jamming the hand with the knife back into the doorframe, where it stuck. He was pretty much defenseless then, held tight and a foot off the floor.

Henry saw the blade fly up to his throat from behind. Duke was carving him deep from ear to ear, like you might take a pig on the farm. He gagged and went limp as the blood poured out in a warm cascade. Dropping him quickly to the tarpaulin spread out on the floor, Duke stood over him to watch. He began to laugh, just a chuckle at first, then loud and derisive.

As his eyes were closing, Henry could burble out just the one question.

"Wh ... why, Duke?"

"Hey buddy," he heard him answer, "I appreciate what you did. Trouble is, there's no such thing as a perfect crime ... when you've got an accomplice. Can I help it if I'm a perfectionist?"

Fading fast to black, Henry whispered: "So this is the thanks I get?"

Duke roared, then crouched down and leaned in close. "You got it, pal!" he said. "That's the thanks you get."

BEACH OF THE DEAD

In 1986, life was going great for Sonny Proulx – until Local 9821's steward phoned Irvin Palazzo on November 25 to ask where Vinny Guyett was. No one had seen the little guy for four days. The Health Insurance Fund was depleted, and the insurance company wanted to know why they hadn't received their check. Irvin wasted no time in phoning Sonny.

"Go see his wife, his mother, his fucking third grade teacher if you have to. Does he have a girlfriend?"

"Christ, Irvin, I don't know."

"Call the crew together. Everybody gets on this. I want his balls in a vise today!"

Until Irvin filled him in, Sonny had no insight whatever into the niceties of mob finance. It seems that Vinny had handled the books for the Local's Health Fund for years. The companies and individual workers who contributed to the fund sent their monthly premiums to a P.O. Box that he monitored daily. After recording the checks in a ledger, he would reconcile the premiums and pay the insurance company on the twentieth of each month – for the previous month's health care coverage. It was all arranged so the members were paying a full month ahead whereas the Health Fund was remitting to the insurance company a month and a half behind.

Once a month, the union leadership siphoned off funds to an investment firm that was actually a mob front organization. This "float" was authorized with the stipulation that an equal amount be returned by the twentieth, in time to issue the check for the previous month's health insurance.

Over time, Vinny must have found ways to game the

system. For one thing, a lot of members and small companies came to him with cash, despite a "checks only" rule. Besides, nothing prevented him from issuing funds to himself or a third party for any administrative expense whatsoever, no matter the size. Making sure everything came together by the twentieth was Vinny's most important responsibility. It also put him in a position to denude the account on the day the premiums were due.

After digesting what Irvin told him, Sonny phoned Red Dalton, one of the thugs on the crew, and laid it out for him. When Sonny finished, Red burst out laughing. He knew who the girlfriend was.

"It's Angela Bartoni, the tall blonde with big hair who helps him in the office two days a week. He told me she makes phone calls and bank deposits. Looks like she been taking deposits too – from Vinny."

By midday, they knew the worst. Angela had told her roommate not to expect her back for a while. Red made the roommate lead him to Angela's closet and determine what she took with her. After checking, Angela's terrified friend was certain she hadn't packed any winter clothes. By then another crewmember, Paul Turnell, had visited Vinny's relatives, including his wife. They all had the same story – Vinny left the previous Friday for New York. He told them Irvin assigned him to meet with the union's national representatives at a conference there.

When Vinny didn't return by Monday morning, his wife got on the phone and found out he never checked in at the Plaza, even though he called her twice during the weekend. Which meant he had kept her off the scent for a couple of days, probably calling from a pay phone as he and Angela got further away. Since today was Tuesday, that gave them a four-day head start.

Sonny, Paul and Red met at the Dunkin' Donuts shop on Vista Drive at three forty-five. They huddled around a table by the big window in back, sipping at large coffees and watching the yellow and orange leaves float down from the trees to the lawn of St. Cyril's next door. Sonny had just placed a box of donuts in the center of the table.

Red: "Fuckin' lemon filling ..."

Paul: "You don't like it, take an éclair."

Sonny: "C'mon guys, we gotta piece this thing together."

Red: "Must be warm wherever they are. We know that much."

Paul: "Bookkeepers got no imagination. Florida maybe?"

And suddenly Sonny had it. Red had figured out the weather angle and Paul was right about Vinny's lack of imagination. But it wouldn't be Florida. Three years ago Vinny took his wife to Puerto Vallarta and didn't stop talking about the place for weeks.

If only Vinny had done something intelligent like lay low in Nova Scotia for a few weeks, then fly to Argentina, they never could have tracked him down. As it was, he made things easy by leaving from the local airport, which is where they found his car. With Irvin's connections, Sonny gained access to the passenger manifests for Friday, November 21. When he found a Victor and Ann Randall booked to San Diego with a four hour layover in Chicago, he figured it was Vinny and Angela. They could have easily gotten a local flight from San Diego to Puerto Vallarta and have arrived on the twenty-second. Maybe a day later if they took a room in San Diego to freshen up between planes.

Sonny expected Irvin to send Red and Paul out there, but he surprised him by insisting that all three of them go.

"Look, I send those two out there alone, I got worries will anybody come back."

"What do we need to do?"

"Vinny is over, Vinny is disposable. Red and Paul will get my instructions about that. You're going to make sure there's no mess and everybody gets on a return flight. The girl don't matter. I know that broad, we'll never hear from her again."

Murder. This was Sonny's worst nightmare, just when he was on the verge of quitting the crew. The things he'd had to do until now were bad enough, but he couldn't help murder somebody. Especially not a poor, dumb slob like Vinny Guyett.

"Hey Irvin, not me, huh?" Sonny begged. "Send Moe Giachetti instead. He won't mind."

Irvin stared at him with those hooded black eyes, compressing his lips and snorting out a puff of air. He wasn't going to budge.

"No, not Moe. You're going, Sonny. Moe's gonna stay and man the office. He'll take payments from members an' let everybody know things are being worked out. You hafta make sure everything goes smooth and quiet in Mexico."

By now they knew Vinny had drawn checks to himself and Angela at just under ten grand a day for about twenty days and had likely put all incoming cash aside for the same period. He got out of town with around $250,000, leaving $95,000 in the health fund – the size of the float returned on the twentieth – which hadn't been enough to pay the October health insurance premiums.

The union big shots were going out of their minds, but Irvin convinced them to shift money from union dues to the Health Fund in order to satisfy the insurance company. If they could hold things together for a week, he promised them he'd get their money back. The important thing was to keep the lid on – no leaks to the press or inquiries from the state attorney general's office.

A major scandal for the union would also involve the local mob. Irvin must have known he'd be the first to fall.

When he sent the crew off to Mexico, he said there was a five thousand dollar bonus in it for each of them as long as the whole episode was resolved without a fuss and with most of the money returned. The way Sonny figured it, fifteen thousand dollars wasn't even a good finder's fee for the cash. When you threw in a murder, it was a positive insult.

~ ~ ~

Late Tuesday afternoon, Sonny made the rounds of travel agents in town and collected brochures on every Puerto Vallarta resort they could find. On Wednesday, the crew split up the brochures and planned to make telephone calls whenever they had waiting time between flights.

In the end, finding Vinny and Angela in Puerto Vallarta was comically simple. Red hit the jackpot on his third call from a pay phone during their stopover at O'Hare. He told the operator at the Hotel Playa Vallarta he wanted to wire a bouquet of flowers to his friends Victor and Ann Randall for their wedding anniversary – they were staying there, weren't they? After a short wait, a reservations clerk came on the line with their room number. The resort was on the beach at Playa de Los Muertos – Spanish for Beach of the Dead. The name gave Sonny a bad feeling, although Red and Paul laughed like hell when he told them what it meant.

"Look," he said, "we wanna keep this simple. We'll stay at the same resort, on the same floor if possible. What's the room number again, Red?"

"They're in 4173. Try to get an adjoining suite. We'll wait until we hear them going at it, then break the connecting door down. Can't ya just see Vinny's skinny ass pumpin' away at that big bimbo?"

"I got a better idea," said Paul. "Break down the door *before* they go at it. You can still check out Vinny's skinny ass, and I'll take the bimbo."

"Fuck you, Turnell."

Sonny knew it wasn't going to be easy controlling these assholes, but he had a plan. First he had to wait for the inevitable. One of them was sure to come up with the idea to keep the money after killing Vinny. Eventually, that idea would fade because they wouldn't be able to come home – ever. Then Red would start to think about skimming off the top before they returned. That's when Sonny would spring the compromise he'd been thinking about. If they could be satisfied with scamming Irvin for a modest amount, he'd agree – but he'd force them to back off their plan to kill Vinny.

~ ~ ~

At the resort, Sonny was the first to spot Vinny and Angela. He couldn't believe it when he checked out the grounds and saw them at the pool. A whole friggin' beautiful beach and ocean just a hundred yards away, and they parked their butts poolside. Looking back to the hotel building, he counted up four floors and scanned the tier of rooms to identify his – where he had tied a t-shirt to the outside handle of the sliding doors on the balcony. From that vantage point, he'd have no trouble observing Vinny and Angela down here at the pool. A simple matter of waiting for them to come back inside. He was glad he'd thought to pack binoculars this trip. They'd come in handy today.

Looking at his watch, Sonny figured he could get back to the room in less than ten minutes. Right now Turnell and Red were checking out the Malecón, the town's seaside promenade. If they returned soon enough, the three of them could put a plan together and might have a chance to corral Vinny and Angela on their way back from the pool. Getting this done in just one day would be terrific, he thought. As long as everything fell into place, they could catch an empty-leg charter out of Puerto Vallarta direct to San Diego late in the afternoon.

As he walked into the vast, open resort lobby, Sonny felt his heart pounding. His flowered shirt, worn outside his shorts, was soaked back and front. The heat was already intense, and he supposed his anxiety made it seem worse. He stepped into the north tower elevator. A short, dark-skinned bellboy in the hotel uniform of red shirt and white pants got on as well, smiled at him, and asked for his floor.

"Four, please."

"Yes, sir," he said. "Me too."

The bellboy was carrying a portable hairdryer with a post-it note stuck to the blower end. Very likely, it had just been handed to him by the bell captain. Sonny could see a number written on the post-it: 4173.

It was an opportunity, but Sonny couldn't figure what to do with it. Should he try to get in the room now? He didn't want to hurt this kid, but being in the room when Vinny and his girl got back would provide a real advantage. His gun was still in his suitcase, though. Even if he overpowered the kid, how would he control both Vinny and Angela with no weapon? No good, he thought, that would never work.

And then it came to him.

"Look son, I think that hairdryer is for my wife Ann. I'm Vic Randall in 4173. Want me to take it for you?"

The young man looked at his note and smiled, just as the elevator stopped on four. "Yes, Señor," he said. "Thank you. Save me the trip."

When the doors opened, Sonny held them back with his foot as he pulled a dollar from his wallet and handed it to the bellboy.

Back in his room, he tossed the hairdryer on the bed and rummaged quickly through his suitcase, finding his pistol and jamming it into his waistband. Next he went to the lowboy dresser and took out the binoculars from the drawer where he had stashed his personal effects. Finally, he hustled to the balcony and brought the pool area into focus, straddling a deck chair and using the railing to steady the binoculars. His pigeons were still there – Vinny with his arm stretched out and stroking Angela's lovely bare shoulder.

Sonny chuckled at the sight. "Cop all the feels you can, Vin. It's gonna be a short honeymoon."

The relentless Mexican sun seared his arms and legs. For the first time in three days, he began to relax. While he spied on his prey, the periodic roar of surf on sand drifted up to him from the beach. Perfect, he thought, everything was just perfect.

~ ~ ~

Turnell and Red got back at eleven-thirty. That was step one. Step two was Sonny telling them how he planned to set up the takedown – by pretending to be the bellboy with the hairdryer.

But Red needed to get something out of his system first.

"Wait a minute, wait a minute," he said. You could hear the doubt and suspicion in his voice.

Sonny had been glued to the binoculars at the railing, but he had to look up now.

"C'mon, Red. We don't have a lot of time. They could start back any minute. What's your problem?"

"I got no problem, Proulx. What I got is a hard-on for Mexico. I can see myself here for a long time. Paul feels the same way. Vinny and his bitch can wait until we get a few things settled."

Well, here it is, Sonny thought. Only trouble being they had an opportunity here they shouldn't blow.

"Lemme see ... " he said, still at the balcony railing and

focused intently on the pool, "you and Paul decided we should rip off Irvin and the union for the two hundred fifty grand and stay in Mexico."

Turnell cut in. "Doesn't have to be Mexico, man."

"Can't you guys see that won't work?" he asked, putting the binoculars down. "You won't ever be able to go back home. You'll both have to stay in big cities down here where they speak English, which is just where Irvin will find you some day. It's not worth it."

Red grabbed his crotch. "Ah, fuck you Proulx. You're not the one gonna get your hands dirty. It's me and Paul gotta do the wet work for five fuckin' grand apiece."

Sonny sat up straight and nodded vigorously to Red. Those were the exact words he wanted to hear.

"And you know what, man? I agree with you. It's bullshit to murder Vinny for five thousand bucks apiece."

Turnell shrugged. "Irvin told us we have to get rid of Vinny."

"He also told us we have to come back with his money."

Red stepped over to Sonny and hauled him out of his chair by the front of his shirt. He pulled him close, nose to nose.

"You're too cagey for your own good, Proulx," he sneered. "You've had some damn thing on your mind since we left. Stop playin' us man! Tell us the big idea and stop playin' us."

Sonny looked him in the eye for a long moment until Red snorted and pushed him away. He righted himself and sighed. If he could just keep it together for a few hours, he thought, he could make his plan work. But unless he managed to placate him, Red would fuck everything up.

"I'm not playing anybody, Red. I've been going crazy since we left because I don't intend to rot in some Mexican jail for murder. And I got no intention to run away – not even for the whole two hundred fifty thousand."

Turnell had been pacing up and down while they argued. Now he stopped, picked up the binoculars, and looked down at the pool.

"Uh, fellas? Looks like we better get our shit together. Adam and Eve down there are makin' a move."

Sonny grabbed the binoculars and checked. "Son of a bitch! We don't have much time."

He turned to them, head pivoting from one to the other. "Can we agree we'll skim off around twenty-five grand and split it? The only other thing is – no murder. Think about it – Vinny already knows he can never go home. Irvin would feed him his own balls."

"Yeah," Turnell chimed in, laughing. "Unless Vinny's old lady got to him first."

They agreed. Sonny didn't care for the look Red was giving him, but they agreed. Christ, if they didn't like the split, he'd give up his own share.

"Paul, go down to the lobby now. There's a house phone in that little alcove off to the left side of the elevator. Call us when they head up. Red and I will time it from there."

"Suppose they go off to the restaurant or something?"

"They won't let them in wearing bathing suits. They might fart around in the gift shop, but I doubt it. Just call if something goes wrong. When they come up, you come up. Check back here first, then go to their room. We'll probably be there already."

Turnell left. Sonny stationed himself at the partly open door, holding the hairdryer. He could see down the hall to the elevators. After a few minutes, he heard a drawer slide open behind him. When he glanced back into the room, Red had pulled his shirt out of his trousers and was fitting his Glock into the waistband at the small of his back. *Shit*, he thought to himself, *I hope he's just planning to intimidate them.* Then the phone rang.

Red answered and listened for a long moment. After setting the receiver down, he walked over to Sonny at the door.

"Paul says they're on the elevator. He's gonna take the stairs up."

That was probably a good idea. The stairwell exit would bring Turnell up into the corridor beyond both rooms. He could make sure the way was clear before he came on the scene.

Sonny raised one arm to signal Red when the elevator doors opened and Vinny stepped out with Angela. They were wearing fuzzy blue bathrobes and holding hands. At the door, Vinny fumbled with the key a moment and shook his head before stopping altogether and putting his arms around Angela.

When they started making out, Sonny grew impatient. He turned to Red, who was behind him and looking over his shoulder.

"Goddamn," said Red, sneering.

Sonny was turning back to look when something caught his eye. Red was holding a leather case in his left hand.

"What's that, Red?" he asked.

Red looked straight ahead and pointed out the door. "Look, they're in. We better do it."

Turnell came out of the stairwell and was right behind Sonny and Red as they walked down to room 4173. Sonny motioned them to the left of the door, then knocked.

"Who is it?" It was Angela's voice.

"You called for hairdryer, Señora?"

"Oh yes. Thank you. Just leave it by the door."

Red groaned. Sonny held up his free hand to quiet him.

"Sorry, Señora. I need you to sign."

"Oh, for heaven's sake!"

"What is it, honey?" asked Vinny.

"Did you ever hear of signing for a hairdryer?"

"That's crazy. I'll get it, babe."

Vinny flung the door open with considerable bravado and a manly look in his eye. But his face crumpled as the crew walked in. Red slapped him once, and Turnell spun him around to hold him with one arm twisted back. Angela fled to the balcony screaming, but Red sprinted after her, tossing the leather case onto the king-size bed as he went. He pried her hands off the balcony railing and dragged her back into the room by her hair.

"It's nicer inside, honey," he said, closing and locking the sliding doors behind them. "You weren't gonna jump, anyway."

"Everybody's gotta calm down," Sonny said. "Vinny, we're gonna leave you alone soon as we have the money."

Angela had stopped screaming. She sat on the floor and stared at Red, obviously terrified of him. Vinny had turned scarlet and was weeping openly. Sonny worried he might be having a heart attack the way he was grabbing his chest with his one free hand.

Turnell pushed Vinny into the overstuffed white armchair backed up against the draperies with the big palm leaf pattern. The rooms were all like that – yellow, green and orange draperies, bedspreads, and wallpaper. If a parrot flew in, it would disappear.

"Vinny," Turnell said. "Just tell us where it is. We'll be gone in no time."

But Vinny was gasping for breath and couldn't speak. The top half of his bathrobe had slipped down when Turnell shoved him in the chair. He sat weeping and helpless with his skinny, hairy chest heaving in and out.

"Your turn, bitch," Red snapped at Angela. "Where is it?"

Angela's pink tongue darted out. "Downstairs," she whimpered, "the hotel safe."

Red had drawn his gun and was waving it. "Oh, Christ," he said. "What fuckin' morons."

Sonny came to the middle of the room. "Okay, we're gonna do this real simple. You're the key, Angela. Everything depends on you now. First, I want all the money you and Vinny kept back. How much you got here in the room between you?"

"I dunno. Around four thousand?"

"Fine, get up and get it for us. And don't hold anything back."

He turned to Red next, wondering how the rest of his plan would go down.

"Look Red, I figure I have to go downstairs with her while she gets the rest of the money out of the safe."

Red's face went tight and his hand came up with the gun. "Why you? Why don't I take her down there?"

"Please don't wave the gun. She shakes every time she looks at you, Red. You scare the piss out of her. They'll know something's wrong if they see her like that."

Angela had collected the money from her purse and Vinny's wallet, as well as an envelope from her suitcase. She brought it all up to Sonny and waited, hands trembling.

"Paul, would you count that?" Sonny asked, then turned back to Red.

"All right, Proulx," Red conceded. "You're right about that. But Paul's gonna be with you, smart boy."

"There's about forty-two hundred here," Turnell said, after fanning rapidly through the stack of bills.

Red grinned at Sonny. "Give it here, Paul. I'll keep this and watch my pal Vinny there while you and Proulx and the bimbo go downstairs and make a withdrawal."

It wasn't what Sonny wanted, but it would have to do.

Two men accompanying Angela was not a good idea. Worse even, what would Red do up here left to his own devices? Poor Vinny was in bad enough shape now – he might keel over and die if Red started in on him.

"Okay, Red, we'll do it your way. Angela, comb your hair and patch your makeup. Then put a dress on – you're going downstairs with me and Paul. What kind of package is the money in?"

"It's a suitcase."

"What'll you need to take down there to prove it's yours?"

"Well, just an ID, I guess. I think I'll have to sign for it."

"They didn't say you'd both have to sign?"

"I ... I don't think so."

"Did you both sign the registry card when you checked in?"

"Yeah."

"All right," he sighed. "Here's what we'll do. Get a piece of paper out of the desk and write something like this: 'I want my wife to retrieve the suitcase we stored in the hotel safe.' Then have Vinny sign it. Just put it in your purse after. You'll only show it to the manager if he needs two signatures."

Turnell began to help Angela. When Sonny caught his breath, he turned to Red.

"I know you don't trust me, but I'm only trying to get it done quiet and right. Help me out, Red ... put your gun away and try to help Vinny calm down. Take him out to the balcony and just talk easy to him, will ya? I think we can be outta here in less than an hour if things don't get screwed up."

Red nodded. "You're doin' all right, I gotta admit."

Now that's a relief, he thought. Red went to Vinny and sat on the arm of his chair, talking to him like an old buddy. Angela had finished scribbling the note and was primping in the bathroom while Turnell waited outside. After a few minutes, Red brought Vinny the note to sign, then walked him out to the balcony. The little guy seemed more in control of himself now. Sonny's eyes strayed over to the bed and that leather case of Red's. He knew he should ask, but figured he'd better leave well enough alone.

~ ~ ~

Angela had cleaned up pretty good. She had all her big, blond hair back in place and had put on a simple silk print dress. A little pale and nervous maybe, but he thought he could talk her into relaxing. When they were ready to go, she asked to speak to Vinny alone for a minute.

"He's gonna bust an artery if he don't calm down," she said.

"Sorry, Angela. You'll have to wait. But he's better now. Red promised me to take it real easy with him. You're the important one, I want *you* to relax. I give you my word you're not gonna get hurt. You and Vinny will have to figure out how to live down here, 'cuz you can never go back home, but at least you'll be alive. We're takin' a big chance too, you know. Irvin ain't gonna be happy if he ever finds out we let you guys stay healthy."

Turnell cut in. "Let's do it, Sonny. I'm getting antsy. This is takin' way too long."

In the corridor outside the room, Sonny turned to him. "Do me a big favor, Paul, and stay back as much as you can. It won't look good with two guys crowding Angela."

"Okay, Sonny. But quick, huh? I got a bad feeling about this."

He didn't want that bad feeling affecting Angela, so he schmoozed her soft and easy all the way down to the lobby. When they walked off the elevator and onto the bright tiled floor, she pointed toward a door behind the reception counter.

"That's the manager's office. I think the safe is in there."

Turnell hung back as Sonny and Angela advanced to the counter and told the clerk to buzz the manager. In a few moments, a pale, dark-haired man opened the door and came out. Sonny thought he was a sort of Hispanic Jack Lemmon with a feverish grin under his little black moustache.

The manager nodded to the registration clerk and looked to Sonny and Angela.

"May I help you?"

Sonny deferred to Angela with a smile. He had been prompting her all the way downstairs and hoped she could perform naturally.

"My name is Ange ... uh, Ann Randall. Room 4173. I have a small suitcase in the hotel safe that I need."

"Certainly, madam," he said, motioning to the clerk and saying something in Spanish. "I'll need your identification and room key, Mrs. Randall."

When Angela handed them over, the manager smiled at Sonny. "And is this Mr. Randall?" he asked.

He gave the manager a warm smile and a little salute. "No, no. Just a friend. Vic is up in their room."

The desk clerk had pulled a card from his file that appeared to be the room registration and handed it to the manager, who made a little bow and walked back to his office.

Sonny was perspiring heavily by now and mopped his brow with his handkerchief. Angela had been marginally credible with the manager, but had begun to tremble again. Turnell was the only one keeping his cool and his distance.

Hoping it might make a difference, Sonny draped his

arm around Angela's shoulders in what he thought was a friendly gesture. She responded with a soulful sigh. Just then, the manager's door opened part way and they heard him screaming at somebody in Spanish. When he came out empty-handed, Sonny held his breath.

"Señora, do you have the receipt we gave you? I could not find …."

"Oh!" Angela began digging through her handbag.

Sonny took his arm off her shoulders then and stepped back. This was going bad … what should he do? He looked at Turnell, several feet away in an armchair, who was biting his upper lip and flexing his arms convulsively.

"Here it is!" Angela said, handing a small tag with a perforated edge over the counter to the manager.

He gazed at the slim piece of cardboard and raised his eyebrows. "This receipt is for the baggage room, ma'am. Whoever took your case misunderstood."

Sonny butted in. "Where is the baggage room, anyway?"

"Over there, sir," he said, pointing across the lobby. "Behind the bell captain's stand."

Angela's high heels clattered across the tiles as they crossed the lobby again. Sonny shook his head and muttered.

"I don't believe it," he said. "Two hundred fifty thou' in the fucking baggage room. Somebody drops a trunk on it … it splits open … Jesus, I don't believe it."

"Oh, Sonny," she said. "I'm sorry. Really I am. The night manager when we got in, you know, didn't speak English so good."

"Maybe he wasn't the only one. Forget it, Angela. Just keep calm."

Sonny took the tag from Angela and handed it to the bell captain, who turned and went into the open room behind his stand. When he returned, he was carrying a black softside suitcase, carry-on size.

"Christ," Turnell said right behind them, "couldn't you at least put it in a hard case?"

"Di'nt have one," Angela whined.

~ ~ ~

Sonny felt drained by the time they got back to Vinny's room. It was one-thirty, time to call the airport about a charter. But the money had to be counted and the skim had to be split. If Red would trust Turnell and him to count the money, that is.

"Look Red," he said, holding the bag up.

Red was strolling into the room from the balcony, behind Vinny. Angela rushed to the little guy, both of them sinking to the bed in each other's arms. Turnell locked the door and waited, hands on hips. Sonny looked for the leather case. It was gone from the bed.

Red's eyes flashed. "It's about time, smart boy," he said. "Everything okay, Paul?"

"Yeh, Red. It was a fuckin' circus, but it's okay now."

"Look, we all know it's taking a lot of time," Sonny said. "We got like five things to do, the way I look at it. We have to count the money and ... Red, get in close, I don't want them to hear."

When Red stepped over, Sonny continued in a whisper. "We count the money, agree on our take and split it, reserve seats on the afternoon charter, tie up the honeymooners, pack and leave."

"Then let's do it."

"All right. After I book the charter, Paul and me can count the money while you keep an eye on our pals. Then you and I can finalize the split. After that, it's a piece of cake."

He should have known coming to a final agreement on what they could skim would tax everybody's patience to the breaking point. He didn't want Vinny and Angela to hear any of it, but how could they not? He hoped they were too worried about their own fate to pay close attention.

Sonny's argument for the split came from knowing Irvin would demand a full accounting of the total amount stolen. Rounding off, that was two hundred fifty grand. Vinny and Angela had spent a measly two grand, leaving two forty-eight. Turnell and Red wanted to skim a total of thirty thousand – ten grand each for the three of them – but Sonny insisted Irvin would see through that just by adding up the figures.

"Look, I can convince him they bought a car down here for say ... twenty-five thousand five hundred. Add that to the two grand makes twenty-seven five they spent. If we bring back ... lessee ... two hundred twenty-two grand and five bills, we can split the twenty-five thousand five hundred left over. That's ... eighty-five hundred apiece."

Turnell rolled his eyes. "Oh man, my fuckin' head hurts," he moaned.

"Goddam, Proulx, if that's what it takes to get you outta here now, fine. Paul and me will take ten grand apiece and you get what's left – fifty-five hundred."

Sonny felt the color fire his cheeks, and he stood up.

"That's it, Red. Whadda you want, gunplay? Well, let's go. C'mon! *Jesus* ... *I* figure it out ... *I* keep us alive ... *I'm* the one has to go to Irvin and sell the story ... and *I* get the short end of the stick? Not fuckin' likely, pal!"

Turnell got up and tried to calm him down while Red laughed his ass off. But Sonny had won the round.

~ ~ ~

At three-thirty, it was time to go. They were packed, and their bags were in Vinny's room. When they left, he might complain to the police that three hotel customers robbed him, but there'd be no trace. Sonny had checked in by himself, and neither Vinny nor Angela knew the

35

number of his room. If the police looked at documentation on departing guests, they'd notice a registration card for Mr. and Mrs. Warren Patterson of Seattle, Washington, occupants of room 4188. The couple paid cash on arrival, but didn't check out before leaving, hardly an unusual occurrence. It wouldn't even warrant a follow up.

Both Vinny and Angela were tied up – Vinny face down on the floor and Angela on the bed. Three packed bags were at the door, plus the carry-on with the money.

"You ready, then?" asked Sonny, eager to start.

Red looked past him to Turnell and nodded.

"Take him down, Paul," he called out, pulling the Glock from behind his back.

Sonny's arms were pinned before he could get to his gun. Turnell kicked his feet out from under him and fell to the floor on top of him, yanking his hair back with one hand while the other twisted his right arm up his back. With his free hand, Sonny tried to reach after his pistol, but Turnell was ramming his face into the carpet, so he used his arm to push up off the floor and try to get over. By then, Turnell had grabbed the gun, rolled off him and was covering him.

Sonny looked over to Red, who had untied Vinny's hands and had him seated at the desk.

"Please, Red," the little man begged. Please ... don't ... hurt ... me."

Poor Vinny was shaking so bad, you would've thought he had Parkinson's disease. Angela must have been able to see from the bed, because she let out a wail that filled the room.

Sonny's breath was coming in gasps, but he kept trying to convince Red to stop what he was doing.

"Red ... you promised," he said, over and over. "You can't ... you can't ..."

"Just gonna get a souvenir for Irvin," Red crooned.

"Nothin' you'll miss, Vinny, don't even worry about it."

Red knelt behind Vinny without taking his eyes off him, slid his left hand back along the floor, and pulled something out from under the bed. It was the leather case. He tossed his Glock to Turnell, who caught it. Standing in tight behind Vinny's chair, Red made him splay the fingers of his left hand on the desk surface and forced his head down so that it was turned away from his hand. Vinny wept as Red adjusted his fingers until they made a kind of fist, but with the ring finger pulled straight out on the desk.

The big guy was laughing as he pulled a meat cleaver out of the leather case. Sonny looked to Turnell, whose face registered fear and disgust. Angela's wail had reached a crescendo.

Sweat dripped into Sonny's eyes and clouded his vision as the meat cleaver swooped up and back down with a thwack. It was over. Vinny was taking huge gulps of air in sheer panic.

"H-u-u-u-u-p! H-u-u-u-u-p! H-u-u-u-u-p!"

His head had come up from the desk, but he stared straight ahead making that awful sound and not daring to look at his hand. Red picked up Vinny's severed finger – wedding band still attached – put it in the leather case and walked to the door where Turnell was waiting. The cleaver was stuck where it landed, in the desk surface.

So Irvin wanted the damn finger as proof Vinny was dead. Only a totally sick mafia wannabe would think up a sadistic trick like that one. Was it because he figured Sonny would try to subvert the order to murder Vinny?

Red and Turnell picked up their bags and the carry-on.

"C'mon, Proulx, we're goin'."

"You can't leave them here like this, Red!"

"Yeah? Watch me, smart boy."

Sonny couldn't believe this was happening. "You

goddamn creep! What in hell's the matter with you?" he yelled over his shoulder as he ran to the bathroom for towels.

"Your choice, asshole. Better not take too long."

Red and Turnell were out the door. Sonny looked at his watch. He needed to help Vinny out, but he still had to make that charter flight at four-thirty. What a fuckin' spot to be in. He snatched the biggest towel he could find from the rack over the commode – a thick white terry cloth bath sheet – and went to Vinny at the desk. The little guy was rocking back and forth, moaning, obviously in shock. The hole in his hand was meaty and red, but the blood flow hadn't really started yet.

Thank God for shock, Sonny thought. He wrapped the towel tightly around Vinny's forearm, wrist, and hand until it made a big ball. Keeping up a chatter for both Angela and Vinny, he made the little guy hold his arm up and grab on to the makeshift bandage.

"Tight, Vinny, hold tight," he said. "We're gonna get you to a hospital."

Sonny worked on Angela next, untying her and telling her what to do.

"I'm gonna have to leave quick, Angela. Get his legs untied first, then call the front desk for an ambulance. There's a hospital in town, they'll take care of him."

"You bastids took all our money!" she yelled. "We got nothin' now."

Sonny's eighty-five hundred was in his bag. He retrieved it and peeled off four thousand-dollar bills, stuffing them into Angela's handbag.

"Oh, that fuckin' Red," she mumbled. "I hope him 'n his kids all get cancer. I hope their fuckin' dog gets cancer!"

While Angela called the front desk and told them she had an emergency, Sonny looked around the room, hefted his bag, and started to open the door.

Angela's blotchy face looked up to him in terror. "Sonny, what am I gonna tell the doctor?"

"I dunno, Angela. The cleaver is right there – tell 'em he was chasin' a gecko and tried to chop it in half."

She grimaced and mashed Vinny's haggard face into her considerable cleavage. "And his hand got in the way?" she yelled.

He shrugged. "Better than if his dick got in the way."

Closing the door, Sonny noticed the red spot on the towel was spreading fast.

A few minutes later, he walked out of the hotel lobby and heard an ambulance siren in the distance. That told him Vinny would get help soon. And he still had time to catch the charter flight to San Diego.

PAYING FOR PAIN

Talley's was the old-fashioned type of city bar Harold favored. It had a long, mahogany counter with a mirrored backdrop. A few dusty prints graced the splotchy plaster walls, and the smell of stale beer and spilled whiskey wafted up from the dirty oak floor.

Harold stood waiting near the door to the back room, a cold bottle of Sam Adams lager in hand, when two guys walked in off the sun-bleached street and took up stools at the middle of the bar. One was a hard case, the other maybe not so hard. The younger guy was yapping away, trying to make his buddy open up. But the hard man wasn't having any.

"Do you believe in anything at all, Chaz? Do you believe in God?"

A pause. "Do you?"

"It don't make sense to me."

"No sense, huh?"

"Hell, no. I don't believe in no God."

"You're sure?"

"Positive."

"Well, I do."

"Sh-i-i-it! You gotta be kiddin'. Tell me about it. Who's God, Chaz? Who's the devil?"

Chaz turned on his stool and thrust his granite jaw right under his pal's nose.

"Ask me who the devil is, I'll tell ya," he hissed. "The devil is every stinkin' surprise that comes along to tweak your tits and grind you in the dirt."

The younger man leaned back, eyes darting around to see was anybody listening.

But Chaz hadn't finished.

41

"Did Daddy slide his big dick up an' down the crack of your ass when you were little?" he laughed. "Some neighbor gal pushed your face in the snow? Does thinkin' about it turn your face red, make your balls shrink up like raisins? That's the devil pal. That's Satan."

Whoa, Harold thought.

The sidekick's eyes bugged out and his chin fell. He tried to cover with a cynical laugh, but it came out lame. When he popped up to stuff quarters in the jukebox and nurse his ego, Harold sent a drink over to the hard guy. Bourbon straight up with a beer chaser.

Eddie Sanchez had told him he couldn't miss the guy he came to see. Eddie was right.

~ ~ ~

They got settled in the back room at a torn-up card table with two rusty-metal folding chairs. Harold had no doubt he'd have to speak first. He figured this guy could stare him down with those agate eyes until he wept spontaneously. But the man surprised him.

"Thanks for the drink," he whispered.

"Sure," Harold said, probably too quickly. "I hope your friend isn't put out that I didn't ask him to tag along."

He shrugged. "If you asked both of us, I wouldn't be here now."

"Strictly a solo act?"

"Depends."

"Depends on ...?"

"The job. My contact said wet work. For wet work, I'm solo."

"Hey ... nothing's that settled," Harold said.

"No matter. You either want me to waste somebody or lean hard. One way or the other, you're paying for pain. You don't have the juice to do it yourself."

Hard is one thing. Stone cold is another. Harold wasn't sure this guy was right for the job. Where the hell did he get off making him feel like that?

~ ~ ~

Harold had grown up with Eddie Sanchez and kept in touch, even as he went to college and his friend wormed his way deeper into the local wiseguy scene. Eddie was the pal you couldn't resist, full of jokes and stories about his sexual and criminal exploits. With him, you came to feel mob associate was a career choice like any other. Not for you maybe, not any more than your old man's factory job was. But nothing out of the ordinary, either.

This was the old neighborhood, after all. Harold may have moved away, but he didn't stay away. And he remembered all of it: the streets, pool halls, alleys, and dives – as well as the nightlife that nourished them. Or was it the other way around? The point is, he wasn't a stranger. His family still lived at 556 West Hanover, second floor rear. He visited a couple of times a month. To make nice with the folks – and to see Eddie.

Sometimes he caught up with him at the garage where Eddie featherbeds on the city payroll, but mostly he called ahead to meet him at Talley's for a beer.

When Harold complained about Carmella that night a few weeks back, Eddie was sympathetic. After all, he'd been married three times himself; he understood the problems a guy could have.

"She cheating on you, Harold?" he asked.

"Nah. Wouldn't matter if she did, though. I could maybe prove it and get rid of her."

Eddie paused. His mouth was wet with beer foam, and his eyes searched Harold's.

"Do you ... uh ... realize you said 'get rid of her'? That what you want?"

"C'mon, Eddie! I was talking about getting a divorce. You know?"

Hoisting his bottle off the bar, Eddie looked away and

smiled.

"Sure ... I know," he said.

That's how it started. Harold wasn't thinking about offing Carmella until that moment. Afterwards, he couldn't stop thinking about it.

Now he wouldn't want anybody to get the wrong idea about his wife. They had some good years. Back in the day, he thought they were made for each other. It's just that her attitude had turned on him. She always had a ton of it, he even liked that about her, but not when it started coming his way. Which it did after she figured out the middle class was the furthest he'd ever take her. No fame and fortune, just an average life in suburbia.

Harold thought their sex life was still hot, even though she made him beg for it. He put up with that because he realized his torture was her foreplay. He would even get into it, crawling up on his hands and knees to lick her toes and sniff her thighs.

Although Harold's chief complaint about Carmella was the disrespect, money had to be a close second. All he wanted was to keep ahead and maybe put a little by for retirement. But when it came to money, they didn't have the same vocabulary. He thought in terms of investments and dividends; Carmella had a penchant for check writing and charge cards.

Eddie had got him thinking, all right. The next time they met, Harold knew he wanted to do something about it.

"Would it be much trouble to put me in touch with a guy if I should want to, uh ... take somebody down a peg?" he asked.

"Take somebody down a peg? What the fuck does that mean?"

"Eddie, gimme a break. I just ..."

"You could maybe hire Rex Reed to make a bitchy

comment and snap his fingers in their face."

Eddie laughed loud at his own joke, punching Harold's shoulder and squinting at him.

Harold pushed him away. "Asshole," he said. "I'm serious. I want to meet somebody ... who'd do anything for money."

Eddie's eyes spread open. Harold could see the network of red veins at the inside corners.

"You *are* serious," he whispered. "Jesus, you really wanna do it."

"Do what, Eddie? You don't know a thing, okay? Just put me in touch."

"Sure, sure. I just never thought ..."

"Don't think."

Eddie slid off his stool and wrapped his arm around Harold's shoulders.

"I got two people in mind, pal. Wanna interview both of 'em?"

~~ ~

The first interview was the hard guy. The second one was a week later. It was well past lunch, and Talley's was deserted except for one old parboiled drunk. He sat propped up at the end of the bar where it curves round – so he couldn't face himself in the mirror, Harold thought.

Like last time, he didn't know a name, just a time to meet. Eddie had told him to look for a tall, good-looking woman in jeans and short brown hair.

"A woman, Eddie? What the hell, man!"

"Think about it Harold. If you was a broad an' a guy comes up to you real friendly, what would you be thinkin'? Guy's tryin' to hit on you, right? Might be tough for him to get close, unless you're in the mood."

"Yeah, I suppose."

"But another broad comes up, admires your shoes, asks where you bought 'em – that's different, right?"

45

"Yeah, but ..."

"Next time she runs into you, maybe you're alone someplace gettin' into your car. She gets close enough to chat – you're not suspicious. Then she snatches you. Get it?"

"I don't know, Eddie. A lady assassin?"

"Please. I thought we weren't gonna get specific."

"Sorry. But, Carm ... my target's no pushover."

"This broad can do it, believe me. She's tough. Gotta be gay, too."

"Christ!"

She walked into Talley's at two o'clock. When the door opened, Harold saw a female silhouette backlit by sunlight. Once inside, the silhouette became a real woman, a very attractive woman, tall and well-built like Eddie said. Her eyes raked the room and settled on Harold. She smiled.

No need for the back room this time. He got a beer for himself and Scotch-rocks for her. They took a table against the wall, far enough away so no one could hear.

Close up, the face was a little worn, and the eyes were cold. Her voice was husky like a female impersonator's. No chance of that, though: hers was a woman's body for sure.

"Did he tell you what the job is?" Harold asked.

"No. Was he supposed to?"

"I want somebody to disappear. For good."

"That's what I do. They don't come back."

"It's a woman."

"Doesn't matter to me."

He nodded. "I would give you a name, address, and description. You would check it out and get back to me through the contact. If we go ahead, we meet and work out the details. I hand over seventy-five hundred up front. When it's over, the contact will have the other seventy-five hundred."

"Works for me."

"She has to disappear, though. If it's botched, I don't know you and I don't owe you."

"You think I'm not a pro, get somebody else. What's this woman like, anyway? She attractive?"

Shit! What was that about? The thought of Carmella getting done by this broad before she got done in pissed Harold off. The worst of it was, he had to wonder if his wife would die happy.

He was beginning to think Eddie Sanchez was screwing with his mind.

~ ~ ~

Despite his misgivings, Harold settled on Chaz, the hard guy. He cashed in a mutual fund to pony up the first seventy-five hundred. When the money changed hands, there was nothing to do but wait. And wait.

It was supposed to get done within a few days. Then Eddie called to say there was a glitch.

"What glitch? For Crissake, her whole routine is shopping, lunch, maybe stopping off at a friend's house. What could be a problem?"

"Witnesses. He says she's always someplace people can see her. But he's figured out a way. Every day she leaves the house twenty minutes after you. He needs you to leave at exactly ten after ten next Wednesday. He'll get it done then."

"At my house? Are you fuckin' crazy?"

"Harold, listen man. You either want it done or you don't. I'm not goin' back and forth any more. I wasn't supposed to know anything, remember? Now I'm in it up to my balls."

"But Eddie, I can't have it done at my house!"

"No, no. He'll just *snatch* her there. Your neighborhood's real quiet around ten-thirty. He'll leave with her in her own car, Harold. What he does and where, you'll never know. Maybe they find her car someday, that's all."

He let out a long breath. "Yeah, all right," he said. "Shit, maybe I should have gone with the dyke."

Eddie laughed. "Told ya, Harold."

On the evening before it went down, he figured he'd be antsy, paranoid even. Instead, things went super smooth. Carmella was in a rare good mood, and they had drinks at home, watched a little TV. Before the night was over, he was slipping her the high, hard one right there on the couch, and thinking how much he was going to miss her sexy side.

About ten o'clock, the phone rang. Carmella picked up. "Hello." A pause. "Oh, hi mama. How are you?"

New York calling, he said to himself. Her people lived upstate. Big, extended family. Harold had met only her parents, who visited one Christmas. The first couple years they were married, Carmella kept in touch, sent pictures, wrote letters. Now there was just the occasional phone call.

When she hung up, she turned to him with a frown.

"Everything okay?" he asked.

"I'm tired, Harold," she said. "Take care of things while I get ready for bed."

"Okay, babe."

She hit the bathroom while he powered off the TV, checked the doors, and turned the lights out. Like Eddie had told him, he made sure the garage door was open. Just before eleven-thirty, he got in bed with Carmella.

Within minutes, she was snoring softly. But Harold was jacked up. He'd never get any sleep tonight, he figured. To keep on course, he forced himself to focus on the negatives – her vicious tongue, the disrespect, the fights about money. No use going all sentimental now. As the night wore on, scenes with torn flesh and severed limbs invaded his scattered dreams. Well, it wasn't like he had a choice any more. He couldn't roll it back now.

~ ~ ~

At breakfast, he didn't eat. The smell of sausage nauseated him.

"What's the matter with you, Harold?"

"Nothing. Upset stomach."

"Well, take something!"

"Nah, it'll be all right in a minute. Listen, the first thing I got at work today is a meeting at eleven. I'm going to hang around here until ten or so."

"Sure, be my guest. Maybe I'll start out early. There's a sale at Adler's I wanna catch."

"Don't rush. Stay with me until I go, Carmella."

Her eyebrows flew up, and she cocked her head.

"Harold, what the hell for?" she asked.

"I just want the company," he said. "We could talk." About what, he had no idea.

"Jesus, Harold, you goin' weird on me?"

Carmella was prickly about it, but she gave way easy enough. They settled in the living room, where he watched cable news and she finished the morning paper.

Two hours passed. At the last minute, he lost track of time. It was ten-twenty when he looked at his watch, grabbed his briefcase, and headed for the kitchen. Carmella was upstairs in the bathroom.

"Bye, honey," he yelled.

No answer. Passing through to the garage, he closed the door and stepped down, turning right toward his car.

The first blow rammed into his neck from behind. Stunned, he fell off the last step and heard his briefcase clatter to the concrete floor. His assailant took him down backwards in a chokehold, sitting him down and forcing his right arm behind his back while he kept up that suffocating pressure at his throat. As the man rolled him over, Harold got a half-second look at his face.

Not Chaz! Oh shit, he thought, this don't make sense. Whoever this guy was had him laid out on the garage floor and was stuffing a thick wool sock down his throat. *Where's Chaz?*

"M-m-m-ph?" Harold tried to ask him, but nothing came out.

"Here's the drill," the voice said. "I've got a gun I don't wanna use. I'm getting off of you now and letting your arm go. The only thing you hafta do is lay there quiet with both hands behind your back."

Harold felt the foot on his spine and complied. Within moments, he was trussed up ankles to wrists and thrown in the trunk of his car. Before the lid closed, a cloth bag came over his head. Rough hands tied the hood around his neck.

~ ~ ~

His shoulders strained in their sockets when the man hauled him from the trunk by his arms, using them like a handle from behind. He hit the ground face first. Ribs cracked for sure. In the distance, there was highway noise. He heard bird sounds close by, and maybe a stream. When he thought of how long it took to get here from his house, he figured they were in the woods outside of town, not far from I-95.

Harold heard the trunk click shut, the car door slam, and the peel of tires. He was alone. His abductor had to be Chaz's buddy in Talley's that first day. *Solo act, my ass!* While puzzling it out, he passed from abject fear to angry resolution. He was still alive, after all. That meant Chaz subcontracted only the takedown. He'd have to show up himself for the – what did he call it – wet work? Then he'd see what a mess he'd made, and Harold could call the whole thing off.

Time passed. The smell of dirt and leaves filled his

nostrils inside the hood, and the sun burned through his shirt. Pain radiated from his neck clear down his arms. Worst of all was the need to suppress his gag reflex. If he hurled behind that sock, he could drown in his own puke.

Finally, a car pulled in – twigs, branches and gravel popping beneath the tires.

When the hood slid off, Harold saw the cynical smirk on Chaz's hard face – like this was a big joke. He held off speaking for a moment after the sock was out so he could clear his throat and suck in the fresh air.

"Think it's funny?" he sputtered. "You gotta be a fuckin' idiot to screw things up this bad. Now cut me loose."

"Can it, shithead," Chaz said. "Somebody wants to talk to you."

The passenger-side door of the car opened, and a long, tanned leg descended to the ground. Carmella! She picked her way carefully over the littered ground and stood looking down at him.

"Thanks for bringing Charles to town, Harold," she said. "That was real thoughtful of you."

"Wha ...?"

"He was just a little suspicious when he met you, thought you might be the guy in the wedding pictures. But hey, all accountants look alike, you know?"

A kind of bone weariness settled over Harold. "Why didn't you just have him do it, Carmella?" he asked. "Why leave me out here like this for hours?"

"Me and Charles wanted to visit, honey. We haven't seen each other in ages. And you needed the fresh air and exercise. You really should get outside more often."

Tears rolled down his face." Carmella, I ... I'm sorry, babe. I don't know why ... I shouldn't have."

"Yeah. I know, Harold, really I do. But just think how poor Charles felt when he saw his baby sister come out of the house that first time. What we decided to do, honey, was rework the contract for you."

She was rummaging through her handbag for something. Chaz had taken a tightly rolled blanket out of the trunk and laid it out to the side of the car.

"I want you to be proud of me for cutting a good deal, Harold. My brother gave us fifty percent off, seein' that we're family. Now I won't have to get up the other seventy-five hundred. Ain't that great? A widow has to watch her wallet."

He saw the pistol emerge from Carmella's handbag. Shimmering sunlight played over the butcher tools laid out on the blanket. How were they going to do it?

Harold swallowed hard. "The gun!" he begged. "Please! First, the gun."

SUMMER OF PORKPIE

KRISTI DARNELL ... We met in South Beach. Yes, it was at a club, but I sure don't deserve that name they call me. Party girl. That's what they say on Page Six of the New York Post when they mean prostitute. It's totally unfair. I may be stuck with it, but I'll never accept it.

I was a model and an actress and I had the credits to prove it. Just local commercials for the acting jobs, but I got modeling assignments all the time. And South Beach modeling assignments are the real thing – great production values, top professionals and good money.

Like I said, we met at a club. I was out with friends when I noticed this good-looking older man watching me. He looked about thirty-two. He was very well built with long black hair, a full beard and the most intense blue eyes I had ever seen. Like most guys on the scene, he wore shorts, sandals and a t-shirt. I never had the least suspicion about his real identity until he told me who he was later on. Porkpie was only a tabloid story to me then, one of those things you read about but never dream you'll be part of.

On that first night we chatted for a while before he bought me a drink. I have to admit I had walked up to the bar to check him out. I've always felt more comfortable with older guys, and I didn't hesitate to take the drink and go out to dinner with him when he suggested it. The girls I was with only laughed when I blew them off and left the club. They thought he was cute too. The name he used was Sam Davidson.

"Is Kristi Darnell your real name?" he asked as we left.

"What a question!" I said. "Did you think I'd give you a phony name?"

"You're an actress – I just figured you might have made it up. That happens a lot, right?"

"Not so much nowadays, but yeah, it's a stage name. My real name is Christy Gore. I hated that. So I changed the spelling of the first name and took the last name from an actress my grandfather used to talk about."

"Who would that be?"

"Linda Darnell. Ever hear of her?"

"No, but I'll bet anything the world will hear about you, Kristi."

Sam was a real flatterer. There was no question he was feeding me a line, but it was done with a friendly smile and you couldn't take offense. Forward motion was his overall method to break down your defenses. At the same time, he was polite and considerate. When you asked him to slow down, he would smile and apologize, but before you knew it he was making another move. Well, when you really like a guy, you don't mind that.

I'm not going to talk about sex with Sam – I think it's awful that reporters and other complete strangers question me about what he was like in bed. And they act as if you owe them all kinds of private information, just because they have nerve enough to ask.

I fell for him real fast. From the first night we met, I think I loved him. He had a way of making me feel completely protected and wanted. I must have needed that. Only twenty-two at the time, I often felt unsure of myself in that world – casting calls, modeling, even the SoBe nightlife could make me feel that way.

Sam moved into my apartment in nearby North Beach soon after we met. He had a little money and we shared expenses. He talked about being a dropout from corporate life on the West Coast, looking for fun and a better way to make a living.

"I broke my butt on my last job, Kristi. I put my heart

and soul into it only to find out I was the only one who cared. That's not going to happen to me again."

"What do you think you'll do now, Sam?"

"One thing I've noticed down here is the tremendous number of boats and yachts. I'd like to be a broker or just work for one as a representative."

Pretty soon, he was making friends down at a marina on Alton Road. A man named Lou Loiselle had a yacht he wanted to sell and Sam was helping him get it into shape. Mr. Loiselle liked to take his boat out into the Intracoastal, but he was getting older and didn't want to bother with the yearly upkeep any longer.

We'd laugh about Lou from time to time because of his mannerisms and his habit of wearing certain clothes whenever he took the bridge – always the blue blazer with the brass buttons and his white captain's hat with the black peak. I thought he was like a father figure to Sam – except for the fact that he was so obviously effeminate.

Besides working on the restoration, Sam did a nice job of describing the yacht for sale. He had fliers printed up and posted around town. Lou was content for the time being to try for a private sale and he promised Sam a percentage if they sold it before he signed with a broker. Sam saw to it the yacht was listed in boating magazines and posted on some Internet sites.

Modeling jobs kept me busy just then, so most days Sam and I would wake up at different times and not see each other until late afternoon. I began to notice how moody he could be and that it did no good to try and draw him out. He could be extroverted and a lot of fun, but in several ways he was the most self-contained person I ever knew.

I would come home to see him lying on the bed, stripped down to briefs and a T-shirt. He wouldn't say a word unless I spoke first. Hands under his head, he would stare at the ceiling, a blank expression on his face. If I got up the nerve to ask what he was thinking about, he might or might not answer.

One of the conversations we had sticks in my mind. It upset me, and I remember thinking that Sam should look for professional help. I came home after a photo shoot and he was stretched out on the bed in the way I just described.

"Are you day-dreaming, honey? You're so quiet just lying there."

"Not day-dreaming, no. Sometimes my thoughts are jumbled up and I think better lying down."

"What's on your mind, Sam?"

"A lot of things. There are people who mystify me, you know? Some folks have a way of judging you while they talk to you, like they're ready to accuse you of something. And you can only wonder about it because they haven't said anything, it's what you're reading in their eyes and their manner."

"Is there someone in particular you're concerned about?"

"Maybe. I don't want to say. I want to put it out of my mind, that's why I'm trying to relax."

"Don't you want to talk to somebody about this? It would bother me something awful to feel that way."

"I'd rather you didn't think about it, Kristi. I'll work through it. It may be nothing. I don't want to blow it out of proportion and get mad. It's not good for me to get angry."

There was something terribly disjointed about the way he was thinking; you could tell he was trying to control it by slowing down. I don't recall being afraid for my own safety, but I was afraid of what he was capable of doing. He was very strong, and when his mood turned you could see his jaw set and his muscles flex. Combined with that intense stare he sometimes had, the effect was unnerving.

Sam had very few clothes for a guy who was in

corporate life previously. He mentioned donating most of his business wardrobe to charity. He did have one rumpled, dirty suit when he first moved in. After a trip to the cleaners, it stayed on its hanger in the bedroom closet. He never wore it that I can recall, just held on to it as a memento of his life in San Francisco. I came to the conclusion that his career had been a terrible failure, and I wondered why he would want a reminder of that.

I was beginning to wonder about a lot of things. When Sam told me Lou Loiselle had died suddenly, I didn't understand why it wasn't in the newspapers.

"Lou's from Fort Lauderdale, Kristi. I'm sure it's news up there. He was just visiting Miami, living on the yacht."

"But you're still going out to the Marina most mornings, Sam. What's that all about?"

"Lou's sister called and told me to keep showing the boat, babe. She wants it sold."

I said nothing to Sam, but Lou told me he had no family left. Could I be mistaken? No, I was sure. And it must have been my curiosity – or my dread – that brought me down to the Marina early one afternoon a few days later.

I only half expected to find Sam there, but he was gone. As I walked down the pier toward the yacht, I ran into Cindy, a middle-aged lady whose husband owned the boat across from Lou's. We chatted for a bit while the bright sun warmed my shoulders and the boats rocked gently in their slips.

Cindy hadn't seen old Lou for a while. She claimed Sam didn't know where he was either. I was kind of freaked out by that, and I cut my visit short before Sam could show up. What could this possibly mean?

When I got up the nerve to question him about it that evening, he looked at me for a long time, then laughed. It was a sharp, rasping laugh, full of sarcasm. For the first time, I felt afraid of my lover.

"I killed him, Kristi. I killed the old fruit. He was drunk and he tried to touch me, wanted to 'know me better' is what he said. I grabbed the fire extinguisher and bashed his faggot head in."

God, the look on Sam's face was awful as he spoke.

"We had sailed around to the Gulf," he told me. "The water was calm, the sky clear. A perfect day, really, until Lou had too much to drink. Then he got way too friendly."

Sam related all this like it was a story he heard somewhere – some filthy, contemptible anecdote that he'd just as soon forget.

Why didn't I run? Why didn't I tell somebody? Instead, I wanted to take care of it for him. For the only guy who had ever made me feel safe and wanted, I thought I could return some of that. This is what I struggle with now – becoming an accomplice to the murder of a dear old man I knew and liked. It seemed to me the greater good was to protect this man I couldn't tear myself away from.

"What did you do with the body, Sam?" I asked.

"I weighted him down with chains and an anchor and dumped him in the Gulf. I don't think there'll be a problem. He's not coming back up."

When we made love that night it was ferocious. The fear I felt mixed in with the excitement of his lovemaking, and I kept telling myself he would never hurt me. No, not me.

I lay in his arms afterwards while he talked about people crossing him, how it made him feel. Suddenly, I thought about that Dolce & Gabbana suit he never wore hanging in the closet. And I remembered the stories in the tabloids about the well-dressed killer Porkpie out west – the big, good-looking murderer who sliced people up and ran away. I knew then I was in love with a man beyond all redemption. How could I get away from him? Did I even want to?

He must have sensed my suspicions about him. The next evening, as we strolled along the beach, he confessed that his real name was Sam Porter, the one the newspapers called Porkpie.

You know the story. He narrated every terrifying detail as if confession might help him understand what he was. I heard about the fuzzy vision and the rush of wind in his ears and the labored breathing. When he got that way, he couldn't stop until he saw the blood flow. Despite his awful crimes, my heart sickened most when he talked about those women in San Francisco – his wife Angela and her notorious sister, Helena Swann.

I had to stop working; the pressure I felt was overwhelming. My life had changed and I wanted to leave Florida. But I couldn't take that first step. Sam seemed to be watching me for signs of – what – betrayal, help?

Then we read the newspaper story about Helena Swann leaving San Francisco for parts unknown. Although she had been Sam's mistress, she tried to expose him before he ran away. The story seemed to hint she might have fled to Europe.

"No ... not Europe," he said. "They're wrong about that. She has relatives up North."

"You're in love with her, aren't you, Sam?" I asked.

"No, Kristi. Maybe I was once, but that all died in San Francisco."

I must have looked confused and unhappy. He drew me close and stroked my face with his big hand and smiled without saying a word.

"Do you love me, Sam? I have to know how you feel."

"My feelings for you are very strong, Kristi, and I want to be with you when I get back."

"Get back? What do you mean? Where are you going?"

"I can't tell you, baby. It'll take about a week. I'll call

before I come home."

But he never did.

~ ~ ~

IVAN CHITWORTH ... It promised to be an interesting summer, although my passion for the dramatic went unfulfilled at first. I was dying to talk about hosting a genuine femme fatale at Dismas Cottage. Regrettably, I found myself required to be evasive and coy about the glamorous blonde from California.

Secrets, like the one I was sworn to keep about Helena's identity, are almost unheard of among my friends. The crowd I run with come from the very best families, complete with trust funds. None of us deign to work, except on our tans. We live for certain social events, play tennis and golf and patronize the arts. Gossip is the very air we breathe.

Newport is a summer thing for my clique. The autumn diaspora to New York and Connecticut is an annual event around Labor Day. I'm one of the few exceptions, having become a year-round resident when my mother sold the New York apartment to move here permanently.

But I was talking about Helena. Her new look was the first surprise. She was blonde now with short, tousled hair. It was more on the order of a makeover than a disguise; still, only a close friend or relative would recognize in her the dark-haired temptress whose photos were on display in all the tabloids. Furthermore, she kept a low profile in Newport. I had expected to introduce her to one or two select friends, but she stayed aloof, intent on keeping herself under wraps. When she had to give her name, she used Helen Chitworth.

Even so, she was the same streetwise gal with the sophisticated taste and sharp wit. Chastened now, perhaps, and wary of calling attention to herself, but it was Helena nonetheless. As she relaxed into the lazy Newport rhythm, we spent many hours together at tennis, on the beach, or just strolling Cliff Walk. I kept the talk light – it's a specialty of mine – but despite my efforts, you could sense a profound gloominess in her mood from time to time.

And what could be more natural than that, after all she had been through? I wasn't privy to her innermost thoughts, you see; I could only look at the awful events in Las Vegas and San Francisco through my own eyes. Having been at her sister Angela's wedding, I knew some of it at first hand.

When Angela introduced me to Samson Porter back then, I nearly wilted under that cold blue stare. He was polite, jovial even, but that look of his went right through me and I thought I could see his opinion of me formulate on the spot: queer. Anyhow, what he thought didn't bother me in the least; I'm quite aware of how I present myself and what people say. My assessment of Sam was also instantaneous: dangerous and sexy beyond words. You go, Angela, I thought.

A few weeks after the wedding, the whole sorry scandal broke. By then, I was back in Newport. The police had connected the dots and everybody was reading Rupert McAllister's sensational story about the murders in Las Vegas and San Francisco. He's the one who called Helena 'Delilah,' and I'm sure you remember the headline that made him famous: **PORKPIE PORTER – SOCIALITE PSYCHOPATH**. McAllister had gotten most of his information from Sam's sidekick Mickey Cullion, the one who ran away to Utah.

Right away, Mother asked me not to talk to anyone about Angela and Helena or our relationship. I thought she was afraid of the publicity, but now I can see she was thinking ahead. When Helena asked to stay with us for a spell, we could honestly say that no one in Newport knew we were related.

Now everybody knows we've seen our share of scandal and mayhem in Newport over the years. Especially, you'll recall Claus and Sunny Von Bulow, and the dark deeds done right around the corner and up the street from us on Bellevue Avenue. To this day, poor Sunny lies unavenged in a coma – a persistent vegetative state, I believe they call it.

Anyhow, the day arrived when McAllister slithered into Newport, and he was determined to meet with Helena. On the night she agreed to see him, I offered to blow off my friends and stay with her. But her expression told me she had other plans.

"Oh, Ivan honey, do go out tonight," she said. "I told McAllister that he and I would be alone."

"Why would you want to be alone with one of your worst enemies?" I asked.

"He knows I'm here and he must want something. So why not meet him on a friendly basis? Depending on what he's after, I may gain some leverage."

It didn't make a lot of sense to me, but I didn't press her. Helena was used to living life on a pretty big stage. She ponders her every move and thinks over the motivations of everyone she interacts with. I can't begin to understand that way of operating; it strikes me as positively Byzantine.

So while Helena was preparing to greet McAllister, I met my friends at eight o'clock in the rooftop bar at the Terrace Hotel. Ten or twelve couples occupied a number of the tables that night. My friends and I – there were four of us – sat at the bar. It was early and very quiet: no one dancing, no one drunk. A reggae band was playing with the kind of shuffling beat tourists seem to like at summer resorts.

Dusk was falling. From the bar, we could look out and

see the old residential and commercial areas that crowd the hill leading down to the harbor. In the fading light, church steeples and the masts of sailboats were just discernible against the dull shine of water.

I must have been quiet for a spell, because Jack Hamel asked if I were feeling all right.

"I'm fine, Jack," I said. "Do me a favor, though. Tell me if the big guy at the end of the bar keeps looking this way."

"You can't be serious, Ivan," he laughed. "This is Newport, after all. People do not come here to cruise."

"More's the pity. But keep an eye on it for me, will you?"

"Sure, if you say so."

As it turned out, I was right. This guy had longish hair and a full beard. He was dressed in shorts, a print shirt worn outside and flip-flops. I took him for a contractor or construction worker who just dropped in for a beer. But he was nursing it, that beer, and soon Jack confirmed that he was looking our way now and then, more often than you'd expect.

So I asked myself the usual questions. Is it me he's looking at? What does he want? Could it be someone who knows me? What should I do to find out? Because I feel awkward when it comes to approaching people, I turned to Jack.

"What do you think? Should I go over and talk to him?" I asked.

"Ivan, he looks like a real bruiser, you wouldn't want to be wrong."

"Well, you know I'm not bold enough to make a play, anyway."

"I suppose you could walk by and say hello if you catch his eye."

"Uh-huh. And then what?"

"On your way back from the men's room, smile and say 'How 'bout those Red Sox?'"

We cracked up at that.

"With my luck, he'd be a Yankee fan," I said.

Soon, I had mostly forgotten about the big guy while the four of us fell into a conversation about Jack's weekend in New York. Later, when I thought to turn around and check, he was gone.

At around ten o'clock, everybody decided to pile into Jack's car for a ride to a dance club in Providence. Everybody except me, that is. I didn't tell anyone, but I was pretty anxious to find out what Rupert McAllister wanted with Helena. If I went to Providence now we'd be out until two in the morning. In that case, I'd have to wait until breakfast to learn what the Tabloid King had to say.

Jack, Tony and Marc said goodbye and left a few minutes before me. I stayed behind to chat a moment with the bartender. When I slid off my barstool and headed for the exit door leading to the elevator, I inhaled the night air and realized I was pleasantly buzzed. Not drunk, just a little high.

Well, I didn't have a designated driver, so I'd have to be careful on the short haul back to Dismas Cottage. I'd be there before ten-thirty. And if McAllister hadn't left, I'd go to my room and wait up for Helena.

As the elevator doors opened onto the lobby, I walked straight ahead to the front entrance. On my left were the bell captain's station, the front desk and a small sitting area. And there he was. The big guy occupied an armchair and was talking with a woman in her twenties. My eyes met his as I passed by. He smiled and said hello, interrupting his conversation.

I could feel the color rise to my cheeks. I needn't have felt embarrassed, but I did. Something stuck in the back of my mind. His voice, I thought, something about his voice.

I would have liked to pull out my glasses for a better look, but no, that would be way too obvious. Actually, I'm too vain to wear them most of the time.

I paused on the front steps a moment before crossing the street to the parking area behind the old Jewish cemetery that faced the hotel. The avenue was lit softly with Victorian-style street lamps. The night air was mild and damp. A mist was beginning to drift in from the harbor.

Traffic was light. I crossed and was into the lot before hearing footsteps. Startled, I wheeled around and spotted him. The level of light from the street behind him obscured his features, but I recognized his form in the semi-dark.

He laughed and spoke up right away.

"Sorry. Didn't mean to scare you. The name's Dave. I'm parked here too."

He had stopped where he was, about six paces away, probably feeling that would enable me to settle down.

"Oh, that's okay," I said. "I guess I got spooked. Don't let me keep you."

He walked into the lot and to my left, car keys in his right hand. Smiling pleasantly, he kept an eye on me as he approached a light-colored Ford Torino.

"Listen," he said, "I'm not from around here. Could you tell me how to get back to the bridge?"

"Yeah, sure," I said.

As I gave him directions, he opened the front door on the driver's side and pulled something off the dashboard. He shut the door and held up a map.

"Maybe you could show me the way on this," he said. "I want to get back to I-95."

I took one end of the map, pointed out where we were and showed him the way. We were standing close now and I was flustered, wondering if – and maybe hoping – he

65

would say something or make a move.

Suddenly the map came down, there was a gun in my face and he was shoving me backwards, against the nearest car. I started to resist, but looking down the barrel of his gun took the starch out of me. His left hand was square against my chest with his whole weight behind it. Instinctively, I had grabbed his wrist, but now I released it and put my arms back, palms outward at the level of my head.

"Good boy, Ivan, good boy," he said. "Take it easy and stay quiet. Everything will be all right."

I wanted to ask how he knew my name, but I was afraid how my voice would sound. I didn't want to beg for mercy or sound like a wimp, so I waited for him to speak again. My breath was coming hard, and soon I would hyperventilate if I couldn't relax. It was then I realized why the voice was familiar. Oh sweet Jesus, I thought. It's Sam, and he's here for Helena!

"Okay, Ivan, I'm gonna let you up now. That's it, nice and slow. Hand over your wallet and your cell phone first, then go over to my car and get in the driver's side."

I could barely think straight, but I surmised he wasn't attempting to rip me off. He must want my wallet for the address, I thought – to find out where Helena is. When we were both in the car, he handed me the keys.

"Drive out of here slowly and turn left onto the avenue."

"Helena's not in Newport," I said. "She's in Boston."

He just smiled and nodded. "Well, I suppose we'll have to wait for her to come back, won't we? I know what – we'll take a ride along Ocean Drive and talk. That's down this way, right? The bartender told me it's real scenic. You must know it."

He was right; I knew it well. The drive meanders along the southern tip of the island. It's a mix of large estates, coves, beachfront and parkland all nestled against the open sea. At night in the moonlight, it's majestic and nearly deserted.

"Why don't you just let me go?" I asked. "I told you she's out of town. I can't do a thing for you."

"Yes you can, fruitcake! You can shut up and drive!"

That made me mad and I wanted to say so, but his eyes were hard and his voice was terrifying. I shut up. I drove.

"Leroy Avenue ... Ivan, tell me exactly where that is from here." He was looking through my wallet as he said it.

I wanted to lie, but we'd be passing it in a few moments and he might easily see the street sign.

"It's up ahead to the left, just a few more blocks," I said.

"Good. Thanks. Pass it right by, we're going to Ocean Drive, remember?"

For a moment I felt relieved, then worse than ever. If he wasn't after Helena and we weren't headed toward Dismas Cottage, what did he have planned? I supposed I wouldn't be long in finding out.

Despite the mildness of the night and the open car windows, my face and arms were covered in a glaze of sweat. My heart had finally stopped racing at about the time we passed Marble House, but my hands still gripped the wheel tightly in an effort to control my shaking.

Bellevue Avenue turns to the west at Rough Point, where the old Doris Duke estate sits sprawling like a medieval castle above Cliff Walk. The moon was high as I made the turn, investing the scene with a kind of pallor that did little to illuminate the darkened roadway.

Two more turns in the road brought us on to Ocean Drive. I could hear the surf slapping the sand on Bailey's Beach as we headed west again. In a few minutes, I saw the sign for King's Beach.

"Pull over here," he said. For emphasis, he dug the gun barrel into to my ribs.

He had me get out first and stand in the roadway next to the car door. You couldn't see the beach from the street, just the sandy path leading to it. Gun in hand, he got out of his side and slammed the door shut. While he waved me toward him, he walked to the back of the car.

"Open the trunk, Ivan," he said.

I fumbled with the keys. I didn't try to use the remote because I couldn't read the symbols well enough. He was getting impatient.

"C'mon – c'mon Ivan. For Christ's sake!"

Again I said nothing. Finally, I inserted the right key and the lid sprung open. He took the car keys from me and told me to stand away a couple of paces. Keeping one eye on me, he shoved the gun under his waistband and groped around in the trunk, pulling out a couple of lengths of rope and a shovel.

He turned to me and smiled as he closed the trunk.

"We're going up that path to the beach, Ivan. You've been real good so far, and I appreciate it. You're not gonna get hurt if you just cooperate. So cooperate."

I didn't believe him at all, although I wanted to badly. If I had felt steadier, I could have run into the trees and brush along the road, but I was so nervous I might have stumbled and fallen. The last thing I wanted to do was make him angry.

As he pushed me along the path, my breathing grew more strained. I staggered forward as stinging sweat poured into my eyes, blurring my already weak vision.

"What the hell ... you drunk, Ivan?"

"I ... can't see too well," I said.

"Yeah, well, we're almost done. Stand right over here on the beach and put your hands behind your back."

While he tied my hands at the wrists, I stood looking out to the ocean and stars. What I wouldn't give to be sailing out there, I thought. I so wanted to stay calm. But what was the shovel for? What was he going to do to me?

"Face down on the sand, Ivan. C'mon, son, do it now!"

My heart was pounding once more as he trussed me up from behind, ankles to wrists. Sand was getting into my mouth and nostrils and my breath came in short and painful bursts.

"The house keys, Ivan, I forgot to ask for your house keys."

He laughed when I didn't answer, probably guessing I couldn't speak to tell him what pocket they were in. When he found them and stood up, everything was silent for a long moment.

Oh Lord, was he pointing that gun at me now? I couldn't see him. When the silence lengthened, I thought he had left. Thank God! But again I wondered what that shovel was for. Finally, what I remember is the sound – *CLANG* – and the blinding pain in my head. Darkness enfolded me.

When I woke up, I was groggy and sick. But the incoming tide was starting to pool around me, and that focused my mind. Struggling to keep my nose above the water line, I saw an old fellow with a white beard coming up the path to the beach. He carried a fishing pole and a bucket. I began to babble and call to him – God knows what I was saying. From the look on the man's face, he must have thought he had found a talking baby whale in the darkness.

His name was Louie. He had come out for some night fishing.

~ ~ ~

HELENA SWANN ... When Rupert McAllister found me out, I knew my grace period in Newport was over.

I had just gotten back to Dismas Cottage from a tennis date with Ivan, who had dropped me off and gone on to a friend's house. I was looking forward to a shower and a quiet afternoon at home. Passing through the side entrance from the porte cochère, I put my racket in the big foyer closet and was stripping off my sweaty headband when Aunt Claudia glided into my field of vision. She was holding her hands at waist level, wringing them slowly. The look on her face was Yankee tragic. Her mouth was drawn down and her eyes sparkled with concern.

"Aunt Claudia darling, what is it?" I asked.

"Rupert McAllister called and left a message, Helena. I told him I hadn't seen you in years, but he just laughed. Oh, what a terrible man!"

"What was the message?"

"I told him it was foolish to leave word since you would never get it. He said 'tell her to call me at the Hyatt Regency,' and he hung up."

Like the replay of a bad dream or the recurrence of a dormant malady, the name Rupert McAllister filled me with dread. For the moment I managed to suppress my fear in order to console Aunt Claudia. I told her there was nothing to worry about.

"But Helena, dear, what will you do?"

"I have to think about it, but I'm inclined to call him. I have to believe he's managed to find me. If it were just a fishing expedition, he wouldn't be right here in town, would he?"

"I suppose not, but what good will it do to confirm that for him?"

"That's what I have to think about. If he knows I'm here and I *don't* call, he'll surely write one of his awful stories and everyone will know. Maybe there's something I can do for him in return for keeping quiet about my stay here ... for now, at least."

"Oh, Helena, are you sure?"

"Please don't worry, Aunt Claudia. I'll think of something."

"Well," she sighed, "would you like of cup of tea, dear?"

Aunt Claudia's offer of tea was her all-purpose remedy, the universal answer to life's woes. So, while she sought out her maid in the kitchen, I went off to shower and change clothes. It gave me a chance to think things through.

The mental ease I was cultivating during those weeks in Newport had already suffered a setback two days ago, when a newspaper story linked the body that washed ashore in Florida to Sam. And now, here was that slimeball McAllister come to torture me.

It was clear I had to talk to him. On the phone, he was unctuous and condescending. With the utmost politeness, I invited him to come visit at eight-thirty the next evening. I made no demands or preconditions. I wouldn't try to negotiate until we met.

"Thanks so much, Mrs. Swann, for agreeing to see me," he said.

"My pleasure, Mr. McAllister. There'll be just the two of us. We'll have drinks and a nice chat."

"Delightful! I'm so looking forward to it."

I'll just bet he was. Aunt Claudia wouldn't present a problem. She had made plans weeks ago to leave for Boston, where she'd be for a few days with a friend in Back Bay. I'd ask Ivan to stay away for a few hours so I could meet McAllister alone. As a matter of fact, that was his routine on Thursday anyhow.

With that settled in my mind, I began to chew over every event and every emotion of the past few months. The only comforting thought was that Sam was unlikely to look for me while so many people were on his trail. His best bet had to be a big city where he could blend in, or perhaps some truly isolated spot where someone could hide him.

Despite my feeling of security in Newport, every newspaper story about his odyssey from San Francisco to Miami put me in agony and renewed my sense of dread. How much of all this was about me? And why did I think these thoughts, why did every new felony and murder seem to form a link in a chain that bound me to him? All I can say is that I never made a mental break with him. Even today, when I awake from a dream about lovemaking, Sam's is the face I'm kissing, the body that presses against me.

Dealing with McAllister would mean answering questions on every aspect of the family scandal. He would certainly want to hear it all: my relations with Sam, what I thought about Angela's pregnancy, what I knew about the murders in Las Vegas and San Francisco – the whole ugly mess. Although I planned to tell him as little as possible, somehow I had to extract his promise not to reveal my whereabouts. Maybe I could trade some future exclusive for his cooperation now.

I certainly wouldn't say anything to him about the jealousy that consumed me whenever my sister's pregnancy came to mind. Oh, *I* didn't want to be pregnant, the thought of having Sam's child was truly dreadful. But her due date! Counting backwards, I realized the child might have been conceived that last morning, before they came down for breakfast ... before he had to run. After a night in *my* bed, he probably impregnated his wife!

~ ~ ~

By the time McAllister arrived the next evening at eight-thirty, I felt in command of my emotions and quite sure I could handle him. I brought him into the living room and motioned for him to sit on the striped silk Biedermeier sofa, while I occupied higher ground in a straight-back armchair. There was a low mahogany serving table between us. We exchanged the usual pleasantries and he gushed about the amenities of Dismas Cottage. I smiled and nodded through this without commenting, just as I had seen Aunt Claudia do a hundred times.

"Will you take a drink, Mr. McAllister? A brandy, perhaps?"

"Why yes, Mrs. Swann, I will. If it's no trouble, that is, and if you'll join me."

"No trouble at all. And of course I'll join you," I said as I crossed the room to the liquor cabinet.

There was a silver tray on top of the cabinet. I took out two snifters and a bottle of cognac from the bottom shelf and put everything on the tray. As I carried it back and placed it between us, I pointed out a box of cigars on the table.

"If you'd like one, I'd be pleased to light it for you," I said. "I won't join you, of course, but it gives me pleasure to see a man enjoy a good cigar."

"Thank you, Mrs. Swann. Absolutely delightful!"

He selected a cigar, took up the little cutting tool and clipped off the end. I was ready with a lighter and he pulled in the smoke with a sucking noise until the ash end glowed. While he watched, I poured a few ounces of cognac into the bottom of each snifter. From his demeanor, I could tell he was succumbing to the ritual. Very few men can resist this sort of thing.

"Now I know we have business to discuss, Mr. McAllister, but I'm hoping we can get to know each other first. If we can talk off the record, that is. I'm very mistrustful of journalists after what's happened."

"I should think you would be. And I do apologize for the sensational aspects of my stories. That sort of thing grows out of not having access to the right people. One can't expect a balanced reportage when the only sources willing to talk are anonymous tipsters and known felons."

Now this was utter bull. The reportage was tabloid style because the story was tabloid fodder, pure and simple. But I went along.

"Yes, I see what you mean," I said. "You know, Rupert, I'd like it if you'd tell me a little about yourself. You're from London, aren't you?"

Well that got him started. Middle class Brits are often uptight with upper class Americans. They feel out of place unless you disarm them with a modicum of respect and an easy manner. Once I had accomplished that, the evening went very well indeed.

He filled me in on his background, and I let him know a few things about my prior life in New York as an actress. Although I made sure we were still off the record, I felt certain this was information he already had by now.

"Did you ever appear in a lead role, Helena? You certainly have the presence for it."

"No, I was neither a very successful actress nor a very good one. I never had a big role, never the kind of success you've had in journalism."

"Really, you know, this story has made me. I can't point to much else."

"Well, you've done a lot with it."

"I suppose so. I've had some luck and I've been resourceful. But there have been ... well, frustrations."

"Such as?"

"You'll pardon me for saying so, but I'm angry that your sister has continued to stonewall me."

"How could she do otherwise, Rupert?"

"Don't you see? Her side of the whole affair could be on the record. All the nasty conjecture would not have been possible."

At least he was consistent with that line of claptrap.

But it was ludicrous. When you go 'on record,' there is that much more room for disputation and innuendo. At this point, though, I thought I might begin to deal with him.

"Well, I'm sure that your business tonight is to ask *me* to go on record," I said. "Still, I don't believe it's time."

"When *will* it be time, Helena?"

"I'm not sure. Right now I feel trapped. You've found me despite my precautions and I'm at a disadvantage. If you tell the world about me, Sam Porter will know where I am."

"There will be no reason to do a thing like that if you can help me, even a little."

"I'm not a rich woman, Rupert, despite what people think. Would my story be worth something?"

"Of course. It could be worth a great deal."

In a few minutes, Rupert McAllister was in a very expansive mood. The cognac refills had done their part also. I had verbally agreed to give him the exclusive story of my involvement with 'Porkpie' for a sum I would negotiate with his publisher. There would be no written agreement for now, and I would not be interviewed until Samson Porter was in jail.

"Why don't I give you a little tour of Dismas Cottage before you leave?" I asked. "You've only seen the rooms downstairs."

It was ten-thirty and I wanted to get rid of him. Ivan would be back soon and I was expecting Aunt Claudia to call from Boston. As we ascended the staircase, I decided to point out just a few things, show him the library and call it a night.

The corridor at the top of the stairs comprises a kind of portrait gallery depicting several generations of Chitworths. While I related a few details from the life of Pardon Chitworth of the Mayflower Compact, I heard a noise downstairs, which I assumed was Ivan opening the front door.

Steering Rupert into the library, I closed the double doors behind us. Ivan knew I didn't want them to meet, and this would enable him to get upstairs to his room unseen. So I was rather annoyed when the doors opened again, just as I was showing Rupert an original New York Edition of the works of Henry James.

I felt a swift expulsion of air from my lungs when I turned and saw it was Sam framed by the doorway, not Ivan. First, there was a moment of grace and confusion while I processed the beard, the long hair, the substandard clothing. McAllister turned to look, puzzled at first. Then his face drained of all color.

Sam's dreadful gaze burned into me a moment before he fixed his attention on Rupert, who threw up his hands and began screaming in a high-pitched wail. When Sam pulled the gun from his waistband, the poor man begged for his life.

"Pl-e-e-ase don't kill me!" he screeched. "Pl-e-e-e-ase!"

He caught up with Rupert in front of the fireplace and slapped him across the face with his left hand. He tried to run, but Sam grabbed him by the collar and kicked him to the floor. As Rupert turned a forlorn and tear-streaked face towards him, Sam lifted the gun, aimed and shot – a look of rage-filled contempt on his face.

I had inched myself over to the doorway. Just as I heard the gun discharge and saw Rupert McAllister's tortured face explode into flying shards of bone and brain, I slipped outside and slammed the doors shut. Because of all the rare books, the library was fitted out with locks that secured it from either side. By the time Sam understood that he'd have to shoot his way out, I'd be gone from the house.

He was kicking furiously at the doors while I raced

downstairs and out the front entrance. The telephone was ringing as I left. Dashing through the grounds to Leroy Avenue, I heard two gunshots from the house. Sam would be after me now.

If I could get to the corner of Bellevue Avenue before he saw me, he'd have to guess whether I turned south towards Marble House or north towards Memorial Boulevard and the town. My lungs hurt from the exertion and my breathing was labored, but I pushed on as hard as I could. My biggest fear was falling and letting him catch up.

At the corner of Bellevue and Leroy, I looked back in terror. Was he in sight? No, not yet. Which way now, I thought, which way? I slipped around the corner to the south and rested a moment, crouching down by the hedge at the boundary of Chateau-sur-Mer, oldest of the large estates on the avenue. Just a little farther south was the entrance gate; I ran to it and hid myself behind a tree inside the grounds. From that vantage point, I kept my eye on the corner of Leroy, where I hoped to observe Sam's approach as he came up to Bellevue.

An eternity seemed to pass. If only I had my cell phone! My nerves were shot and I was afraid I wouldn't get far if I had to run again. I strained to listen, but my breathing was the only thing I could hear.

If he had gone the other way, I thought, it might be possible to sneak back home. I darted back to the gate and peeked around it to see if he had turned north on Bellevue. My eyes took in the glamorous heart of gilded age Newport: the endless row of Victorian street lamps, wrought-iron gates and high protective bushes – all bathed in misty, amber moonlight. No sign of Sam.

Oh, but there he was – not thirty feet away – just south of me on the *other* side of the street! When he saw me, a grim smile spread across his face and he raised the gun. In a blind panic, I stumbled out to the sidewalk before righting myself and dashing back up the driveway toward the chateau. I meant to run a zigzag pattern, but the shot he fired whizzed past my ear and drove me straight ahead.

Moments earlier, I had seen a flash of light when I peeked around the entranceway. But it wasn't from his gun. Maybe I was beginning to hallucinate a little from nervous tension. There it was again, and again. Now, still running, I heard another shot – followed by searing pain. I dropped to my knees on the asphalt and fell face forward, panting.

Sam was shouting my name in a hoarse voice I hardly knew.

"Helena! Helena! I'm here, bitch!"

But there were other voices too, and a barrage of gunshots. Pop! Pop! Pop! And still I saw the flashing lights. When I heard footsteps pounding up the driveway, I was prepared to die. At the final moment, you know, it just doesn't matter as much as you thought it would.

"Miss? Are you all right?"

A young policeman with schoolboy looks knelt beside me. I understood then what the flashing lights were about – his squad car.

"I've been shot," I moaned.

"An ambulance is on its way. I'll stay here with you until it comes."

"Did you catch him?" I asked.

"We took him down, Miss. He's dead."

"Oh."

"He mumbled something before he died. It sounded like 'Delilah.' Do you know who that is?"

"No," I whispered. "No I don't."

NO GOOD DEED

A Novella

Meet Mickey Cullion, at one time Sam Porter's best friend. Years have passed, and the summer of Porkpie is a distant memory for most. In San Francisco, however, they remember.

Against his better instincts, Mickey has come back to the town he fled all those years ago. The very same town where Helena Swann lives in her sister Angela's imposing Marina District home.

Not frequenting the same social circles, he'll surely never run into them ... will he?

Porkpie is gone, but the legacy lingers on.

CHAPTER 1

When Michael Lester Cullion got out of San Quentin in late 2001, he had served a little more than two years for felony embezzlement. If he hadn't been very lucky, the charge might have been accessory to murder.

During the long months in prison, Cullion thought hard about his way of life. What tortured him at trial had been the District Attorney's insistence that he was a career criminal. Well, if that were true, he had to come to grips with it. He needed to understand himself and the things he had done.

Jim Hendrickson claimed to have an answer for him. He was a kind-faced preacher who came to the prison twice a month to conduct bible lessons. Seeing an opportunity to start over, Cullion joined his group. But even with all Pastor Jim's help and mentoring, he couldn't claim to be born again. Still, he felt a commitment to Jesus, and he prayed daily for spiritual guidance. Unlike other men who attended Jim's classes, he didn't exult in his newfound belief; instead, he felt truly humble before his God.

And he had his share of problems. His proclivities for sin and crime hadn't disappeared; he only kept them in check as best he could. In a way, he was glad for his difficulties. How would he know he was a better person if the path was easy?

Maybe it had been a hard life, but he had to own up to making it that way himself. He remembered how his uncle stressed a man's being judged by the company he kept. Well, Porkpie Porter had been the worst possible company, yet he stayed with him for five years. Five years, because he had an unnatural attraction to the man; five years that ended in multiple murders and Cullion's own throat cut.

For the embezzlement from Sharples Communications that Porkpie had planned, Cullion went to prison – and, yes, he deserved it. He hadn't participated in those murders in Las Vegas and San Francisco, but he did help Porkpie get rid of evidence. He admitted nothing to the authorities on that score, thus avoiding more serious jail time. This was another wrong, he realized, another sin to expiate. But he just could not have done years and years of hard time again. He hoped to be forgiven for this weakness.

The important thing now and tomorrow was to live his life differently. In the short term, this meant two things: keeping his head on straight and staying out of San Francisco. One way to keep his head straight was to insist on his own worth and dignity. He might be a little guy, but from now on he wouldn't respond to nicknames like Mickey and Weasel, tags he had been saddled with all his life. He was Michael now – or Mike, he supposed that would be okay. Leaving San Francisco behind was important because of the terrible associations it had for him. He hated the town. Good thing he had permission to serve his parole in Idaho, where he grew up and where there was a job waiting for him on a grounds crew.

The landscaping work didn't last long when he got to Boise, but he soon found a job washing dishes and managed to scrape along from week to week. He kept his appointments with the parole officer and attended services regularly at an evangelical church. Still, the nights were hard. The spirit may be willing, he told himself, yet the flesh is eternally weak. He didn't kid himself, however; he knew it would be like this.

Three years passed that way. Then the letter came, filling him with hope and driving him to despair by turns.

The sentiments were right, the situation was totally attractive ... but he'd have to leave Boise and return to San Francisco. The town he swore he'd never set foot in again. It was Pastor Jim writing to tell him he had established a storefront church in the Mission district and could use his help.

Well, he sure was struggling to make ends meet in Boise. And here was Jim offering a place to stay – telling him he could take a full-time job days and just help out weekends and evenings. This was a totally decent man whom he loved and admired, under whose tutelage he had come to Christ. So he said yes, saved for a bus ticket and went three weeks later. On the move again with no possessions, leaving behind even the beat up thirteen-inch color TV and the old Mr. Coffee that he thought of as his two luxuries.

~ ~ ~

Pastor Jim and his wife Betty were there at the bus terminal to meet him. They had warm smiles, and they each hugged him in turn. He hadn't met Betty before, but Jim had talked about her so often that he felt he knew her. Jim insisted on carrying Cullion's beat-up suitcase out to their car.

"Allow me, Michael," he laughed. "We're counting on your help, so we're determined to treat you like a prince from the get-go."

He watched them from his vantage point in the back seat as Jim pulled out into traffic. They were old enough to be his parents – late sixties, he figured. Jim was tall and slim, but rangy and powerful looking behind that lively, open face and pleasant smile.

By contrast, Betty was short and heavyset. Everything about her said housewife and mother from her braided hair to the simple dress and her deferential manner. Michael knew they had only one child, a girl who had died from leukemia at age six many years ago.

When they arrived at the Breastplate of Faith and Love Mission, he paused on the sidewalk and glanced in the direction of downtown. They weren't too far past Market Street. This was his neighborhood in 1999 when he worked at Sharples Communications. He sighed under the weight of a burdened memory.

The storefront church was a bit shabby outside, but he was sure he could help put that right. It was a small, two-story building sandwiched between decrepit apartment houses and had probably been built as a retail establishment of some sort. There were two large plate glass windows on either side of a recessed doorway.

Once inside, his spirits lifted. A second ground-level door to the right of the storefront accessed the Hendricksons' apartment. They walked into a narrow entranceway with a staircase to the second floor. Upstairs, their rooms were spacious and pleasantly, if sparely, appointed. Skylights filled the interior with sunshine. The ceilings were at least ten feet high.

When Jim and Betty showed him to his room, he was moved. It was evident they went through a great deal of trouble to make it nice for him. Jim seemed especially pleased to show him the separate entrance that led from the back of his room to the narrow alley between the building and the apartment house next door. It was his way of telling Michael that he could have as much privacy as he wanted. Yes, he appreciated that. Jim handed him a set of keys and looked him in the eye.

"This is your home, Michael," he said. Betty was just behind him, looking on with a shy smile.

"Thanks, Jim," he said. "And thank you, Betty. Thanks a lot."

He stopped speaking then and turned into the room, not wanting them to see the tears that were springing to his eyes.

"You're welcome, son," Jim said. "Your suitcase is right here. We'll leave you now to get settled."

"We're having supper at five o'clock, Michael," Mrs. Hendrickson said. "We'd be pleased to have you join us."

He murmured his thanks again as the Hendricksons retreated, closing the door behind them.

CHAPTER 2

Cullion tramped all over the downtown area for three days looking for messenger work or anything else he could do, and it wasn't happening. The one job offer that came his way was dishwasher in a restaurant on Market Street. Same ol' shit, he said to himself. Why can't I rise a little higher than this? But he took it. The red and blue neon sign said Continental Diner. His boss was Theo, the elderly Greek who owned the place. Trying to keep things positive, he told himself this was a start. After all, he had a place to stay for free. Minimum wage wasn't so bad when it was mostly spending money.

It *won't* always be like this, he promised himself. He'd find something better so he wouldn't be living off the Hendricksons. For now, though, having a comfortable room and good people to share his life with gave him a sense of family for the first time ever. Maybe it was a little suffocating, their daily concern for him and everything he did, but it was better than the dog-eat-dog scene he'd been through for so long. It was damn nice just to have a conversation without having to figure out the difference between what was said and what was meant. These folks said what they felt. Sometimes it made him stop and wonder; it was hard to shake the mental reservations, the cynicism that had been second nature for so long.

One Tuesday a few months later, Carlos, the Latino short order cook, walked off the job during lunch. He had been bickering with one of the waitresses for days and blew up when Theo called him on it. Cullion watched as the old Greek pulled an apron out from under the counter and took his position at the grill, wearily scanning the orders propped on the stainless steel frame over the

87

exhaust hood.

He had been at the other end of the counter, consolidating the cleared plates and cups into one plastic tub, when the drama took place. After a brief, stunned silence, the conversation level ratcheted up again. The patrons had seen and heard enough by now and were getting back to their meals. A tight, nervous feeling in his stomach told him to make a move. He could do that job; he knew he could.

He moved quickly with the tub of dishes, tucking into the back room through the swinging doors. Except for this little batch, he was caught up. Putting the tub down, he wheeled around and walked out front.

"Theo," he said. "Gimme a chance, man, I can do this job for you."

"You can do breakfast, lunch, sandwiches, the whole thing?" Theo looked pretty doubtful.

"If you could help me a little the first couple days getting used to the way the girls order, the way they write it down – I know I could."

"Mike, who's gonna wash dishes?"

"Right now I'm caught up. I'll do what comes back for lunch after the rush. Or you could spell me out here when it piles up. Ah, c'mon Theo!"

Theo was grimacing and shaking his head, but he turned and looked at him when he heard the urgency in his voice.

"So, you want a chance at this. Okay, take my apron. Here. Cook! You do good, I'll call the agency for a dishwasher tomorrow."

He already knew where everything was, no problem there. Theo stood with him the first day and read the orders until he got the hang of it. He didn't get panicky when the order slips piled up mid-lunch, but Theo stepped in anyway to do sandwiches and salads whenever he got behind. As he promised, he went back and did dishes after the rush, staying on with the second shift until they were caught up.

Although he went home with knots in his stomach that first day, he didn't stop to feel sorry for himself. All night, he kept thinking how he might do better. The first week had its ups and downs, but he got through it, learning technique quickly and staying in good temper. By week's end, Theo was smiling and saying "good boy, good boy" every time his shift ended. It was a producer's job and he had learned how to do it. He was proud of himself.

Contributing money to the Hendrickson household gave him the sense he was in control of his life for the first time ever. Jim and Betty listened to his stories each evening like parents happy for a son on his first job. The mission work was also going well. Evenings and weekends, Cullion did handyman work and helped Jim with newcomers, especially younger men who had criminal histories or involvement with alcohol and drugs. As often as not, those things went together.

Occasionally, he would even give witness about his life and how he had come to Jesus. However awkward it felt to speak out, he managed to convey his experience honestly, and Jim praised him for it. Of all the work he undertook, he was most at ease when painting. Sprucing up the storefront was a real pleasure. He loved the way the dark, rich blue color gave new life to the gold-tone lettering on the picture windows: Breastplate of Faith and Love Mission. He repeated the name over to himself. It was from Saint Paul, he thought.

It was good to be busy. But he had ... feelings that never left. Sexual longings that tortured him. Maybe if he dated that waitress Julie – she was about his age. But he wasn't sure how that might work out. He should take it as a challenge to his faith, the way he felt. If he couldn't master it, he would have to live with it, would have to keep in mind how bad those old choices were for him. If only he could talk to Jim Hendrickson about it. By now, Jim knew everything about his past except for his attraction to men and how he had helped Porkpie after the Las Vegas murders.

He really *could* tell him, he thought, because Jim would listen and try to help him. There was no doubt about that. And maybe he would tell him, except that he was afraid to hear Jim say he should go to the authorities and confess. Besides, how do you talk to a guy like that, someone with all the old-fashioned manly virtues, about your sex preferences? No, it wouldn't work. They'd be too embarrassed – both of them.

In the end, he found he needn't have troubled himself about it. And he shouldn't have come to rely so totally on his mentor's good opinion of him. It had all been a waste in some respects. Jim Hendrickson died suddenly, and a world of trouble opened up before Michael Cullion's eyes.

CHAPTER 3

The funeral service for Pastor Jim was simple and brief. Cullion took two days off work and did everything he could for Mrs. Hendrickson, helping her arrange the cremation and details of the service. He was surprised at the cremation, figuring most Evangelicals frowned on it. But Betty knew her husband's wishes. The only thing he saw as a burden was her request that he give the scripture reading at the service. He stayed up half the night thumbing through his bible, before he hit on a passage he thought Jim would appreciate.

At Betty's request, a friend of Jim's flew in from Minnesota to conduct the service. His name was Hugo Swanson, and he spoke of Jim's life in plain and heartfelt terms. The story of Betty and Jim's early bereavement over their daughter was especially touching. Cullion was sitting in the front row with Mrs. Hendrickson. She had insisted Jim would be proud to see him there in the position a son might have taken. But he felt too small and stupid to fill those shoes. He thought everything about himself was inappropriate to the occasion, including the double-breasted blue suit he found at the thrift shop.

When it came time to get up in front of the congregation for the reading, he was terrified. He sat there fidgeting until he heard his name and saw the expectant look on Hugo's face. Betty gave him a little pat on the back as he rose to take the lecture stand. He placed his bible there, open to the passage from Acts, wet his lips and forced himself to look up. It made him feel a little better to see Theo in the back with Julie, the waitress from the diner. Nice of them to come, he thought.

The silence was beginning to feel oppressive when he

finally spoke. His voice sounded reedy at first, although it improved as he went along.

"*And when they had eaten enough, they lightened the ship, and cast out the wheat into the sea. And when it was day, they knew not the coastline, but they discovered a certain creek with a shore, into the which they were minded, if it were possible, to thrust in the ship. And when they had taken up the anchors, they committed themselves unto the sea, and loosed the rudder bands, and hoisted up the mainsail to the wind, and made toward shore. And falling into a place where two seas met, they ran the ship aground, and the forepart stuck fast, and remained unmovable, but the hinder part was broken with the violence of the waves. And the soldiers' counsel was to kill the prisoners, lest any of them should swim out, and escape. But the centurion, willing to save Paul, kept them from their purpose, and commanded that they which could swim should cast themselves first into the sea, and get to land: and the rest, some on boards, and some on broken pieces of the ship. And so it came to pass, that they escaped all safe to land.*"

~ ~ ~

Towards evening he took a long walk around the city, dropping in at the diner on the way back. Theo was sitting in a back booth, going through receipts and making notes on a yellow pad. Cullion slid into the bench opposite and waited until the older man looked up.

"I'll be in tomorrow, Theo. Thanks for coming today."

The old Greek nodded and pointed to the east.

"I been thinkin' all day, Michael. That was Saint Paul landing on Malta you was preachin' about this morning. I don't think I ever heard it in English before. It made me think how far I am away from home."

Cullion smiled. "Welcome to the club, Theo. I always feel that way."

"Julie was very proud with you. I could tell."

"I'll have to thank her for coming, too."

"You should ask her out, Michael."

"Really, now? You a matchmaker, Theo?"

"A-a-a-ay. Old people like to see young people together. They know it stinks to be alone."

~ ~ ~

Mrs. Hendrickson must have figured it stinks to be alone, too. A few weeks later, while showing him the monthly bills and collection receipts, she told him she needed to go home.

"That's good, Betty. You should take some time."

"I ... don't think you understand me, Michael. My relatives in Minnesota want me to come live with them."

"Oh," he whispered. What else could he say?

"I know you can carry on Jim's work, Michael. He would have wanted that. You're needed here at the mission."

"Both of you showed a lot of faith in me. But I don't know, Betty. I want to keep my job at the diner. And I'm not a preacher."

"Keep the mission open, Michael. At first you could operate a couple of evenings and weekends. When you do find a preacher to help, you can resume a daily schedule. It will work out if you try."

Everybody was giving him advice lately, and they all meant well. And change was supposed to make you feel this way, right? Maybe he just lacked confidence. Remember those knots in your stomach, he thought, when you first took over the grill? You were determined then, and you got through it, didn't you? Sure, but running a mission and working full time, and trying to stay straight – could he really do all that?

It occurred to him that he had always been a follower and that he wanted to remain a follower. But now he was being challenged in another direction. Keep the job, get a girlfriend, run the mission. Be a man is what they were saying. Well, he'd pray on it, but all the prayers he could say would only help him make a decision. They wouldn't guarantee his decision was any good.

The first problem he needed to solve was making sense of the evening services. He pared down the format to just a reading, a theme, and some witnessing. The collection was pathetic at first. He was no Pastor Jim who attracted all kinds to the mission. Some guys and a few gals were coming, mostly alkies and druggies, mostly looking for a handout. And it was harder now to keep on top of the maintenance; he didn't always have the time. But he had to admit it was rewarding; somehow he felt Jim's spirit at work in this place. The Breastplate of Faith and Love. He repeated it to himself often, like a mantra. The image made him feel secure.

Cash flow, too, was a problem. The Hendricksons held a small mortgage on the building, and Betty agreed to let him forward a check to her every month in return for keeping the mission going. She could have sold the place at a profit, but Jim's work and memory were more important to her. Cullion figured he could swing it by renting the second floor apartment while keeping his own room. And it wasn't long before an immigrant couple with a young child took him up on the notice he posted at the mission. This was stopgap financing at best, but he was keeping his head above water.

When Julie Reyes starting coming to weekend services, he took the plunge and asked her out. She was so shy about accepting, he was afraid he had made a mistake. Later, she admitted that Theo had hounded her into making a move; her shyness came from her fear that she had somehow trapped him into dating her. He took her to a movie the first time, and they went out for coffee afterwards. When they walked back to her place, he held her hand. She was so petite and cute she made even a little guy feel like a big man.

Gradually, they fell into a routine that had him going to her tiny apartment every evening to watch television. He liked her, really liked her, and she was satisfied with him sexually. He tried to feel good about that, but old desires still haunted him. In the end, every sex act with Julie was kind of frustrating for him. Would celibacy be better than this? He couldn't really say. Change was tough – that's all he knew.

CHAPTER 4

Cullion watched the new guy slip into a back pew during a Thursday evening service. He was a rugged, good-looking man in his mid-thirties – dressed in jeans, t-shirt, and a brown leather bomber. He had a quiet, self-assured air as he looked around the hall. Jake Snider, he said to himself. He knew him from prison.

Luis, an elderly gent with a patched and dog-eared bible, was reading a long passage from Job. You might have thought he *was* Job with his hangdog look and the plangent whine in his lightly accented English. But Cullion was always grateful when someone volunteered to read. He was leaning against a table to the side of the hall and listening to Luis when Snider walked in. Rather than be spotted there, he moved into the nearest pew and sat until Luis was finished and the witnessing had ended.

Julie always set up the Fellowship Hour, the euphemism Jim had concocted for donuts, coffee, and chat after the service. But tonight she was gone to Santa Rosa to help her sister, who had just had another baby. Before leaving, she promised Theo and Cullion she'd be back on Monday. So he had spent the necessary time setting things up tonight: brewing coffee in the big urn, making a run for donuts, and putting out chairs for anyone who might want to stay and talk when the service ended.

He knew it was just a self-conscious fantasy when people told you they could feel somebody staring at them from behind. In prison you got the feeling often, mainly because it was hard to keep your nose clean with all the warring factions. You were always on edge, or at least he was. Outside, the feeling gradually faded away. But tonight, he swore he could tell where Jake was every second. And when he turned around to look – he was right. Although he didn't catch him looking back, not even once.

When he was set to close up, however, Jake walked up to him grinning, as though he just realized who he was.

"Hey, Mickey, this your gig?"

"Uh, my name's Michael, pal. What's yours?"

Jake looked at him, smiling still, and seemed to make a careful mental adjustment.

"Well, sure, it's been a long time. I'm Jake Snider."

His hand was out and Cullion shook it.

"Oh yeah, I remember you. Well, like I said, my name's Michael, Michael Cullion."

Jake paused another moment and held his look.

"No offense, man. Just thought I'd say hello. See you around, Michael."

He watched Jake leave. He was satisfied the guy respected him for bringing him up short like that. Jake had been a notorious wolf in prison, but he hadn't ever hit on Cullion. Then again, "Mickey" Cullion's old prowess with a knife had helped keep the wolves away in San Quentin.

~ ~ ~

It was Sunday morning and Cullion felt terrific. For once the sun was out early and poured in through the diner's windows. He had walked over from his room at five o'clock to open up. Julie was still in Santa Rosa, but the other two waitresses – one a fill-in – came in on time, and things were ready to fly by six-thirty. Theo probably wouldn't come in until noon, when he would spell Cullion for the last hour and close the place around one o'clock. By then, he would be at the mission getting the Sunday service started.

Brenda unlocked the front door a little before seven when the first patron showed up, a regular who would want a short order of French toast with extra butter. The two slabs of bread were dipped and on the grill before the customer sat down in his usual booth by the entrance. Soon the place was filled, and Cullion was deep into his routine. The air was thick with customer chatter and the heavy diner smells of strong coffee and breakfast meat.

The first, brief slowdown occurred around ten-fifteen. The noise level dropped, the orders were caught up, and Cullion had a chance to clean the grill before the next wave. Ready to take a breather now, he turned around to look out at the street and found himself staring directly into the eyes of Jake Snider, sitting hunched over a coffee at the counter just in front of him.

"Well, Reverend, you're a busy, busy man. Spiritual mentor, expert short-order cook ... any other talents I should know about?"

Jake was busting his chops, but he was smiling good-naturedly. There seemed to be a hint there about something else, but that could be his defenses working overtime, he thought.

"First time I seen you in here, Jake. You in the working class now?" he asked, stripping a pair of latex gloves from his hands. He pointed to his blue work clothes with the "Jake" patch sewn onto the shirt.

"Sad to say, bro, sad to say. I caught on part time with the maintenance crew at the Pinney building across the way. Sundays I get the duty until one. I'm gettin' by, y'know?"

"Yeah, I guess I know how that feels."

"I saw your a___ ... I saw you there flipping jacks when I was walking by, so I figured I should say hi."

"Good, Jake. I'm glad you came in. Can I get you something to eat?"

"Uh, no. Truth be told, I'm a little short ... Michael."

The guy seemed to be on his best behavior, maybe

even a little lonely.

Cullion stepped to the grill. "C'mon, Jake, name it. Bacon and eggs?"

"Okay, Mike, but I'll pay you back. Over easy, wheat toast. All right if I call you Mike?"

"Mike is fine. Bacon and eggs, over easy!"

At noon, Theo came in and relieved him right away. He ditched the apron, grabbed his windbreaker off the clothes tree next to the lockers, and left by the rear entrance, coming out to Market Street through the alley.

While he walked over to the mission, he tried to organize his thoughts. Jake was big and damn hot looking with the buzz cut and the full, dark beard. He had no idea if he could trust this guy, but he hadn't come on to him, and he seemed to have completely dropped the wise-guy routine Cullion remembered from stir. He didn't ask Jake where he lived, but after seeing him at the Breastplate and now at the diner, he figured he lived in the neighborhood somewhere.

Shit, he didn't need this. It would tear down everything he was trying to build if he got involved with this guy. Then again, what did he have really? A ton of responsibility, damn little free time, and a feeling he was just faking it, never making it. His love for the mission's work was real, and so was his feeling for Jesus. But his longings and his weaknesses were real, too. Best to admit it, he thought. And now that he had – how the hell was he going to deal with it?

As the service wound down around two o'clock, Jake walked in and slipped into the same back pew as on Thursday, dressed once again in jeans, t-shirt and leather bomber. If he had time to change from those work blues, Cullion thought, he was living nearby all right.

Why couldn't Julie be here today? That would have saved him, he figured. Jake was outside the mission waiting for him when the service was over and everybody was gone. Even so, all Cullion had to do was go out the back way, take the outside stairs, and go up to his room. Jake had no idea yet where he stayed.

Instead, he walked outside, locked the mission door, and strolled over to where Jake stood. They spoke quietly for a few minutes and went up to his room, where they spent the afternoon.

CHAPTER 5

Jake Snider lived at a halfway house and wouldn't be eligible to move out until he had a full-time job. That took some pressure off Cullion for the time being. It served to keep just a little distance between them, although Jake came around often. Poor Julie, she thought it was nice he had a friend. She even asked him to bring Jake over to watch TV and have a beer, but he said no – he didn't think it was a good idea. So Julie and he still saw each other, even though their physical relationship had deteriorated. How long was she going to put up with that, he wondered.

The very first thing he straightened out with Jake was his complete lack of interest in drugs or criminal activity. "That stuff is behind me, pal. I can't live with those vibes, and I can't ever take another stretch in stir."

"Hey, Mike, I swear I don't want that either. First off, I gotta get out of the halfway joint. After that, I'm gonna try to make it straight. I'm not as sure of myself as you are, but I'm doing what I have to day to day."

Well, it was good enough for now. He figured Jake really *was* doing the best he could. Besides, the guy helped out with the maintenance chores at the mission. In fact, he did a lot of them now, even though the mission's tight budget wouldn't let Cullion pay him more than a few bucks over materials' cost. Jake was a much better plumber and electrician than he was, all of which gave him a little breathing space in his schedule for the first time since Jim's death.

He thought of Jim often. It was his own joke with himself that WWJD stood for What Would Jim Do. Hell, he knew Jim wouldn't be making time with no guy, especially an ex-con. One thing sure, though – Jim's old struggle with finances couldn't compare to what he was going through, the paycheck-to-paycheck crunch with absolutely no daylight. Jake's view, on the other hand, was that Cullion had practically made it to the middle class. What a hoot! Finances aside, the thought plagued him that he had traded away the spiritual basis for his life. And for what?

One evening when they had finished painting the hall, the last of the planned improvements, Jake asked him about Porkpie. It was a sore subject for him, and he hadn't discussed it in a long time, except with Jim Hendrickson. When he glanced over at Jake, he could see he was just cleaning a roller and probably had no idea it was tough for him to talk about it.

"Ah, why do you wanna know, Jake?"

"Christ, Mike, it was a helluva big case. I'm just curious."

"The thing is, nobody here knows I was sent up for that. Theo doesn't know and neither does Julie. They know I was in stir for embezzlement, but that's all."

"Hey, I'll back off. I'll even forget I know you're connected. How's that?"

He shrugged. And then he started to talk. He must have needed to. And he didn't stop until he let it out, all the old fear and excitement and soul-sick misery. Jake stood slack-jawed, taking it all in.

"They called him Shoo-fly when we met in stir. Which he didn't like – his name was Sam Porter. After I got parole, we hooked up and landed in Vegas. Like a jerk, I helped him get rid of evidence and leave town when he butchered that gal Lana and her boyfriend. In San Francisco, he did it again – sliced up an old woman who guessed he was the killer.

"By then he was married to Angela Sharples, the society lady, and I was working for him – helping him take money from the company she owned. Any man should have been satisfied with Angela, she was gorgeous. But no, he had to be screwing her sister Helena too, a snotty bitch who wouldn't give you the time of day.

"Of course, I shoulda known my turn would come. He cut my throat and left me for dead, probably figuring he was getting rid of the last person who could tie him to Vegas. It was a helluva mess, except that I wouldn't die. I even squeezed him for a payoff so I'd shut up and leave town. In the end, Helena turned on him, ratting him out when the police were closing in. Only Angela stuck by him. Without her help, he would never have gotten out of San Francisco.

"The press had a field day, especially this one reporter McAllister. He had it like Sam was Bundy and Cunanan and Dahmer all rolled into one. Anyway, he made it down to Florida under a different name, grew out his hair and a beard. Then McAllister runs a story that Helena left San Francisco and nobody knows where she was. But Sam must've remembered she had relatives up north.

"When he got to Newport and found her with McAllister, he had to be totally freaked out. He shot the guy's face off and went after Helena, even managed to put a cap in her. Before he could kill her, though, the cops took him down."

Jake shook his head as though he could hardly believe it. "Jesus, I know I never heard it like that!"

"Nobody has. Nobody. If the cops knew everything, I'd still be serving time and Helena would be in for a stretch besides. She delivered the payoff to shut me up. And a private dick told me he got money from Angela and Brad Styles, the guy she married later."

Cullion could tell that Jake was stunned. Right away, he began to wonder if he had said too much. But when Jake didn't follow up with any questions, he felt easier. He had fallen for this guy, no doubt about it. And if you couldn't talk to your lover, who the hell could you talk to? At this pass in his life, he needed to confide in someone.

Neither of them spoke for a while. Cullion was kneeling by a ladder and folding drop cloths. When he finished cleaning the rollers, Jake pulled off his white coveralls and walked up to him, ruffling his hair and squatting down to meet him at eye level.

"Look, I gotta get back to the house early tonight. See you tomorrow."

"Oh. I thought we might go upstairs for a while."

"Yeah, I'd like that. But the house honcho told us to get back for a meeting at seven."

Cullion said he understood, but he had counted on Jake staying with him. He needed someone close, especially tonight. When he blew off Julie earlier in the day, he used the painting project for an excuse. But she wasn't having any, and got all teary-eyed.

"Ah ... c'mon Julie," he groaned. "What's wrong now?"

"You don't love me!" she wailed. "I don't think you can even stand me anymore."

It was a bad scene and he was too embarrassed to defend himself. After letting him have it, she walked away. He should probably call her, but what would he say? He got red in the face just thinking about it.

CHAPTER 6

Jake left the mission because he was on to something and had to mull it over. Just when he thought the Reverend Weasel had reached the end of his usefulness, a new wrinkle shows up. That stuff about the socialite dame playing bag woman for Porkpie had given him an idea. And maybe, just maybe, there was more to the story than that. He remembered something about Angela Porter having a baby – that kid would be older now, say seven or eight years old. Those people were some of the richest in California, and you could bet they didn't like publicity. Yeah, there must be an angle or two here someplace.

All that crap from Cullion about 'Michael' versus 'Mickey' burned his ass. The only reason he hung around at all was he figured there was money to be had at the mission. But shit, weasel-boy was honesty itself nowadays. He'd probably call the police if a day's collection money ever disappeared. Another thing – Cullion was getting way too sentimental about him. Hell, a little guy like that was okay when nothing else was available, but he wasn't his damn lover. And now that Cullion was neglecting Julie, he figured on making a move in that direction sooner or later. Some people couldn't see the forest for the trees, he thought. Well, that was okay. Advantage: Snider.

When he got back to the house, only three guys were in the common room playing cards. There was no meeting; he made that up to get away. In his room, he flicked on the overhead light and sat thinking. Then he stripped, grabbed a towel, washcloth, and bar of soap, and headed to the bathroom.

As soon as the water began to run warm, he stepped into the shower stall and let it cascade down his chest.

Slowly, he lathered himself: trunk first, then arms, then legs. Next he soaped up his washcloth and strung it across his back, shimmy fashion. Someone had left a sample bottle of shampoo on the inside shelf, so he worked a dollop into his scalp and beard. Finally, he let the water do its work, running freely until he was warm and lethargic, and totally relaxed.

When he felt clean, the thoughts came. It always worked that way. After getting dressed, he went down to the common room to find a pen and some paper.

"Writing home to the folks, Jake?" the counselor asked, grinning.

"Oh yes, professor," he deadpanned. "Father forgot to send my allowance this month."

The guys playing cards cracked up; the counselor shook his head and went back to his magazine.

When he thought about it, Jake figured he might find everything at the library. They'd have computers there for one thing, and he might need to look at some old newspaper articles. Recalling what Cullion said, he wrote down the names and dates he was sure of. Then he read everything over carefully, underlining words as he went along: *Helena, child, tabloid story, $$.*

~ ~ ~

In the morning, he went to the library and signed up for computer time. While he waited for an opening, he asked a severe-looking Asian lady at the research desk about back copies of newspaper articles.

"You'll need microfiche records for that," she explained. "Do you have the names of the newspapers and the exact date ranges you're interested in?"

"Not yet, but thanks. I'll get back to you after I do some work online."

The Internet search went well; in an hour he had a couple pages of notes and decided that was enough. On a last minute hunch, he browsed through the true crime section and found a book by Rupert McAllister – *From Las Vegas to Newport: The Porkpie Saga*. The dust jacket said the book was posthumous, taken from the reporter's extensive notes and interviews.

Now this is interesting, he thought. Maybe he could misfile the book a few rows above, apply for a library card, and come back for it later. But he didn't want a library card – and he didn't want to wait. When he decided the security system might be based on embedding something in the book cover, he held the pages tight in one hand and yanked the cover free. Because it had a barcode strip and pocket, he ripped the first page off as well. Finally, he spotted a security strip on the spine and peeled that off. He slipped the remaining pages into his jacket, filed the cover where the book had been, and started back to the halfway house. If he still triggered an alarm, they could chase him.

Reading McAllister's book later that night, Jake realized he had what he needed – he wouldn't have to go back for microfiche records. It took him more than a week to outline the story and make a list of the things that only Cullion knew. He had to keep seeing him to flesh out the story. Not wanting to make him suspicious, he never asked more than one or two questions at a time.

Eventually, he put it all together. First, Mickey Cullion was accessory after the fact to the Las Vegas murders. Second, a private eye named Brunetti tried to blackmail Angela to hide what he knew about Porkpie. Brad Styles stopped that, but still gave Brunetti five grand to tell *him* the story. Third, Helena Swann carried a payoff to Cullion from Porkpie, which made her his bag woman and a possible accessory after the fact to the old lady's murder in San Francisco. Finally, McAllister never met with Cullion, like all the stories said. What really happened was Brunetti found him, got the whole story and sold it to McAllister.

This stuff was news; nobody had covered it before. And he figured it made Angela Styles vulnerable. She was rich and publicity shy. Most of the story involved her family, and it hit her sister pretty hard. Releasing it in the right place would focus the spotlight on her and her little boy just when her life was back to normal. It might be worth money to quash it, a lot of money. He thought the best approach was to write a story tabloid style and get it in front of her somehow with a demand for maybe twenty grand. Damn, he couldn't write for shit, but it looked like he'd have to learn.

The newsstand in the building where he worked carried the kind of tabloid newspapers he wanted to study. After reading a few, he saw why people bought the stuff. The stories were laid out quick and nasty, with a lot of insinuation. You might not believe all of it, but it was fun to read. And you nearly always got a real negative opinion about some big shot who should have known better. So that was what he had to do: give a real bad impression about Angela and her sister Helena in five hundred words or less. They wouldn't want to see themselves that way, and Angela would pay to prevent it.

He spent hours writing and rewriting the story. He knew it wasn't perfect; maybe it was no good at all. But he had gotten the point across. Angela Styles and Helena Swann would look like hell if this got published. Jake was proud of himself for a job well done.

CHAPTER 7

Jake watched the ballroom fill up with ladies and gents in eveningwear. A lot of these dudes must be on their second or third marriages, he thought. Lots of trophy wives around. He could swear the average age difference was twenty or more years. Sure, you could find couples with matching gray hair, but it was mostly salt and pepper – or half-bald – for the guys and blond for the gals. Even more characteristic was a paunch for him and pumped up boobs for her.

Nevertheless, the cut glass chandeliers sparkled alike on everyone, and dozens of amber-colored sconces spread a sweet honey glow wherever you looked. Outside the ballroom windows the whole city was lit up. This was a class affair. And why not? With Angela Sharples Porter Styles as the hostess, that was a foregone conclusion.

He had seen the notice in the newspaper she owned, the San Francisco Record. The annual Charity Ball and Dinner for Alzheimer's Research. And he would have passed right by the announcement if the name of her company, Sharples Communications, hadn't been displayed in bold letters. It was society page stuff, with Brad Styles's picture and hers – the perfect San Francisco power couple. A thousand-dollar-a-plate affair. Well, he figured the catering company would be looking for waiters. And he was right.

His uniform fit him nicely. Gray vest, black bow tie, white shirt, and black pants with a satin side stripe. Some of the waiters didn't look too professional in their black sneakers, but he was wearing a proper pair of leather pumps. He knew the sharpest looking guys would have a chance at the better tables, so he trimmed his beard carefully and made sure the outfit was spotless. He didn't expect an assignment to the head table, though. That would probably go to those with the most experience, the ones the maître d' felt he could trust.

It worked out pretty good. One of his tables was within fifteen feet of the place settings designated for Mr. And Mrs. Brad Styles. Close enough to scoot over at the right moment and hand the lady an envelope. At which point he would disappear from the hall.

Half way through dinner, a hotel functionary approached Brad Styles and whispered something to him. Styles got up from the table, spoke to Angela a moment and walked away with the man. This was it. Jake delivered the drink he was holding, tugged the envelope out of his shirt pocket, and walked over to the head table – directly in front of Angela Styles.

Man, this lady is a knockout, he thought. She smiled graciously as he stood before her and held out the unsealed envelope across the table. Slowly, her eyes shifted down to look at it.

"Yes? Who is this from?" she said as her hand went out to take it.

"I wouldn't know him, ma'am. He said you'd want to read it right away."

"Very well," she said, her smile fading.

He walked quickly through the ballroom and out to the caterer's staging area in back. In the hallway, he took the service elevator to the ground floor and left the hotel by the back entrance. He had pulled it off. And he doubted that she had looked at him close enough to describe him later. They could never trace him because he gave a phony name and social security number. He wouldn't be looking to get paid anyway. Not by the caterer.

~ ~ ~

Angela Styles pulled out two typewritten pages from

the envelope the waiter handed her and started reading. As the color rose to her face, she stopped and retrieved a pair of reading glasses from her purse. It was like some vicious tabloid story written by a fourth-grader with a rudimentary sense of spelling. But she knew almost all of it to be true. Rather than read it a second time, she looked around to see where the waiter was who delivered it. Gone. She sighed and looked for Brad, spotting him with Cesar Beragon, a famous vintner and an old family friend. Quickly, she folded the pages and stuffed them back into the envelope. Brad didn't have to see this, she thought, at least not right away.

It took all of her composure to get through the dinner, give her speech, and start the ball with Brad. She couldn't very well leave early, either; she would be the focal point of the receiving line at evening's end. In the meantime, the conviction grew in her that she must take care of this by herself. If it was the wrong thing to do, what in God's name was the right thing? What she had in mind was certainly worth a try. There was no choice, in fact, when you thought about it. She had to keep that story out of the newspapers if at all possible.

When Brad and she got home, Angela claimed exhaustion, took a shower, and went to bed. It was after midnight, but she wasn't in the least sleepy. She was lying in bed thinking when Brad came into the darkened room, drew the covers back, and climbed in next to her. Probably assuming she was asleep, he put his hand on her shoulder and kissed her gently before turning to his side of the bed. Within five minutes, he was snoring.

Angela got up slowly, making her best effort not to disturb him. She took her robe from the chaise by the window and pulled it on. Watching Brad sleep for a moment, she suddenly thought of Justin and walked down the corridor to his room. He lay there, small against the queen-size bed, a trickle of saliva running from his mouth to the pillow. As always when she checked on him at night, the bedclothes were in disarray, all but one leg uncovered. She stood by the bed, pulled the covers up, and tucked him in. If she kissed him he might wake up, so she resisted the impulse.

Instead of taking her evening bag upstairs when she came home, Angela had shoved it into the drumtop drawer of the huge foyer table. She knew she would come downstairs later to fetch it – precisely as she was doing now. The pink and clear glass beads sewn onto the white satin bag glittered briefly in the moonlight as she walked across the foyer and into the library. She sat heavily into a wingback chair facing the fireplace and turned on a lamp. Then she sighed and pushed her long blond hair back from her face. Finally, she opened the bag, slipped on her glasses and reread that loathsome ... thing.

Infamous Porkpie Sequel

It is said by many the case is closed. But we have found it is not. There is more to this tail of the society psychopath and his many loves. In the first instance, you may be surprised to know that Mickey Cullion was accessory in the Las Vegas killings for helping Samson "Porkpie" Porter burn evidence (his clothes) and getaway. He was only sent up for embezzlement, one of Porkpie's ideas.

But the most shocking of all new facts is the involvement of those San Franciscans of great prominence. That would be Angela Sharples Porter (now Styles), Helena Swann, the sister, and Brad Styles, who is now married to Angela.

Did you know a private detective name of Pedro Brunetti tried to blackmail Angela for thirty grand? Well, you do now, because it's true. Brad Styles got in the way of this development, but he still gave Brunetti five grand. Not a bribe maybe, but just to tell what he knew. Still, this was not published before.

If this was not enough, just wait for the biggest news of all. Helena Swan was Porkpie's bag woman as well as his mistress! She carried a bribe from Porkpie to Mickey Cullion so he would not tell all. The big idea was to shut him up after Porkpie killed the old lady, Wanda Buckley. This makes her an accessory too, because she must of known what the bribe was for.

One more thing you never knew. The big time reporter who made the case famous never interviewed Mickey Cullion like he said. It was the private detective Brunetti who found Cullion and sold the story to McAllister (who died too).

To Mrs. Styles:

I'm sure you would not like to see this in the newspapers, on the front page. It doesn't have to happen either. All I want is twenty thousand dollars in twenties and fifties. We need to do this in a public place with no police or other people. I have a copy of this in a friend's email file, which gets sent by him or her to the Chronicle if I don't come back on time. This will hurt you and your family – just what you don't want, I'm sure.

Have the money in one or two big envelopes held in front of you Thursday at noon exactly, right by the entrance to the Cutliffe building on Market Street. If you are not there or if anything happens to me, the email goes.

Do this right. I'll know you when I see you. You don't know me. I'll come near you and say Are those for me? And you'll hand them over. That's all.

This was no professional, she could see that. And

whether that would prove better or worse for her, she couldn't know. But he wasn't asking for much and probably didn't have many resources for following up. The format of his blackmail letter was quite clever ... but the execution! Still, she had to admit he had pulled a lot of information together and uncovered some embarrassing facts. And approaching her that way at the charity ball showed real ingenuity. Was the waiter her blackmailer, or was he only the messenger?

She had an idea that whoever it was could be cowed. If she gave him what *she* thought was reasonable and told him she'd involve the police next time, he'd probably leave well enough alone. But how would she get this message across? If he were going to snatch the package and run, there'd be no time for chat. Well, she could put a note in the envelope, couldn't she? Just as he did. A note saying here's half of what you demanded, and you'd better be satisfied with it. If I hear from you again, my husband and I will work tirelessly to have you apprehended.

This was *not* about saving ten thousand dollars, she thought. It was about showing this creature who's boss. Yes, she could be tough when she had to be. She'd muddle through this somehow, but ... was it true Helena worked with Sam as an accessory to Wanda Buckley's murder? The old suspicions about Helena's relations with him flared up. She had never accepted the innuendo foisted on the public in the tabloids, even though .... Yes, that old hurt retained its power; she felt it like a wound opening up under pressure.

CHAPTER 8

Helena Sharples Swann was the figure people remembered most from the days of the old Porkpie scandal. She was Angela's racy stepsister who had devolved into the Black Widow, Sam Porter's femme fatale. Finally, she became his victim when he tracked her down in Newport and shot her, just before being taken down himself in the last scene of their sordid drama.

Now she was the lady in the wheelchair, victim of her own concupiscence, seldom seen but instantly recognized whenever she ventured out of the Marina district mansion. Putting aside all that had happened, Angela and Brad provided and cared for her in the very home she had disgraced.

Despite the paralysis in her legs, Helena kept up appearances. Her clothes were up to date, her makeup always fresh, her hair faultlessly cut and groomed. If she were a poodle, she'd be a champion. She sometimes felt like a family pet, in fact – the way she was stroked, fed treats, and encouraged to do little tricks for her mistress. Oh, she supposed that was an exaggeration, the bitter spirit of a woman crippled at age twenty-nine. Conflicted feelings aside, she tried to be thankful for the life she led with Angela and Brad since returning to San Francisco.

But there was a kind of watchful truce between her and them, especially between her and Angela. The world saw her stepsister as goodness personified. She had always had a reputation for unaffected elegance, a kind of remote but admirable innocence. Of course, if Angela ever heard a description like that, she would certainly have denied it. Her self-image was one of probity and tenacity – unglamorous and old-fashioned.

117

Perhaps only Helena could reconcile these disparate portraits. Day after day, she sat in her wheelchair and observed: Brad, her former fiancé; Justin, son of her heart's ruling passion; and Angela, queen of all she surveyed. She always loved her stepsister and still did. Yet there was this tension between what Helena felt and how much she resented her own fall from grace. And it colored all her relations.

Today, however, was not a day to sit and brood over complicated relationships. It was Thursday, the day after the big charity ball, and she wanted to hear all the details. She had been invited, as always, but her presence at any society event was problematic. Photographers would show too much interest, and the best people would drift away with raised eyebrows and whispering God knows what. So it was prudent to stay away from the functions and parties favored by her old crowd. The few friends who remained loyal after the Porkpie *scandale* came to see her at home.

This year she had assisted Angela in planning the dinner and ball. Starting last Monday, she helped her rehearse her speech. Helena actively enjoyed these duties; they gave employment to her mind. In addition, they led to a proprietary feeling about the affair. So it was natural that she was anxious to hear all about it this morning.

But Angela didn't come down to breakfast.

"She left early," Brad said. "She woke me up at six-fifteen to say she was getting an early start – something about business in town and getting to the bank at nine o'clock."

"That was all?"

"I think so. I was so groggy I went right back to sleep. I suppose she'll call either or both of us later."

For now, there were just the three of them. Helena sipped her morning coffee and watched Justin devour a plate of blueberry pancakes. At eight-thirty, Brad left for work while Helena waited with her nephew for the tutor to arrive.

~ ~ ~

It had threatened to rain all morning, and the moody skies were just now letting a light drizzle sift through the cloud cover. Jake Snider stood on Market Street across from the Cutliffe building – close enough to watch the front entrance, yet far enough away to make it unlikely he would be spotted. As other pedestrians were doing, he stood near a bus stop under the awning of a retail store. When he saw the blond lady in the pink raincoat standing to the left of the Cutliffe's entrance, holding some kind of package, he flipped his cigarette into the gutter and walked to the nearest crosswalk.

His heart was thudding in his chest while he waited for the traffic light to change. He took deep, slow breaths to stay calm. If this went right, it would be his first decent score ever, and who knew what else might come of it. But don't get ahead of yourself, he thought. Stay focused, stay on target.

That morning, he had shaved his face clean. On his walk downtown, he put on sunglasses and one of those baseball caps with an old man's gray ponytail sewn in. Just before leaving the halfway house, he had taken somebody's cheap nylon windbreaker from its hook in the front hall. He was satisfied that no one would get an accurate description of him, even if a camera caught his action.

Angela was gazing squint-eyed down the street as he drew near the building's entrance. He walked by her and into a soup and salad joint with a front door just beyond where she stood. The restaurant had a second entrance, he knew, that led directly into the main building's foyer. She'd be expecting him to approach her from the street, so he figured to come out of the building and surprise her. She'd have less time to study him that way.

Angela held the big envelope against her chest with her arms crossed in front. The sidewalk was thick with noontime strollers. Jake walked up to her from behind and tapped her shoulder. She spun around, looking tense and uncertain.

In a curt voice, he said, "Are those for me?" and snatched the envelope from her, walking away into the flow of the crowd. The next few seconds would be crucial. His building was adjacent to the Cutliffe, right on the street corner. He turned there and sprinted to the service entrance, looking to see that no one had followed before opening the big steel door.

Once inside among the ladders, trash barrels, and discarded boxes, he ditched the windbreaker, sunglasses, and baseball cap where he could find them later. Then he took the old service elevator up two flights, crossed a corridor, and walked back down to check in for work. A buddy of his had punched him in a half hour earlier, a favor he'd have to return some day. He was still breathing hard, but smiling, when he got to his locker and changed into his work clothes. His leather jacket was there from yesterday, along with a duffel bag. He set the envelope down behind the bag, then closed the door and spun the combination lock. Golden, he thought, he was golden.

~ ~ ~

Helena was on the terrace speaking to the housekeeper when Angela got home a little before one o'clock. Right away, Esther hurried off to assist her. Through the French doors, Helena watched as Esther took her sister's purse and raincoat. Angela glanced at Helena, but made no move to join her. Sensing something terribly wrong, Helena directed her scooter toward the entrance. But Angela raised her arm with a palm-out gesture, signaling her to stop. She walked onto the terrace, carefully closing the doors behind her, and passed Helena

120

without looking. When she reached the glass and wrought iron patio table, she stopped and looked out at the bay.

While Helena remained speechless, Angela covered her face with her hands. Her first tears spilled through trembling fingers and fell soundlessly, until she had to gasp for air. After that, she wept freely.

"Oh, Angela, what's wrong? Tell me what happened."

Helena rolled up and reached for her hand, but Angela rebuffed her and turned away.

"It's starting over again," she said. "Someone is blackmailing me."

She had placed a small envelope on the table, which Helena didn't notice. She picked it up now, pulled out the sheets of paper, and dropped them in Helena's lap.

"You'll want to read this," was all she said.

Helena felt the blood rise to her face almost instantaneously. When she read the sentence that accused her of being an accessory to murder, she was furious.

"No!" she screamed. "No! Who is doing this? Who did you meet with today?"

Angela turned to her with a strange look on her flushed face.

"Never mind that," she said sharply. "I took care of it. I gave him ten thousand dollars and a note to let him know there won't be any more. But your outrage won't do, Helena. What don't I know? What did you do with Sam that morning before he ran off?"

"He shot at me, Angela, remember? It happened right in front of you that day. How can you think I would have helped him murder anyone?"

"It doesn't say that, exactly, does it? It says you carried a bribe to Mickey Cullion to help Sam. Is that part right? Well, is it?"

Helena had wheeled around sharply, away from Angela's gaze. She couldn't bring herself to speak again just yet.

"No answer," Angela said. "Oh, I wonder what that means. Have you ever been truthful to me about anything, Helena? What other things don't I know?"

"You don't know the things you don't want to know, Angela. That has always been your way."

"Must I point out that I have very definitely asked you a question that I *do* want the answer to? And I'm waiting!"

Angela was pressing her close, and Helena had to recognize that she wouldn't back off.

"Yes, all right! I never told you or anyone that Sam asked me to take a package to Mickey Cullion that morning. But that doesn't make me an accessory to murder!"

"What does it make you, Helena?"

"What are you getting at! Haven't I suffered as much or more than anyone because of Sam Porter?"

"Oh, I won't even try to answer that. We'd probably need a jury to decide. But you're stalling for some reason. I want to know right now what you did that day and why!"

For the only time in her life that Helena could remember, Angela was implacable, relentless.

"I hated Mickey Cullion," she said wearily. "You know I did. He called me up the day before to say that Sam had hurt him. He was demanding the money Sam owed him to shut up and go away. He said he'd tell all about Las Vegas otherwise. You know yourself we thought Sam was involved in casino fraud, not murder. That's why you thought Brunetti contacted you – and that's why I thought Cullion was contacting me. Sam gave me a package to deliver to him, and I did it. I didn't think you had to know. And I didn't tell the police because it looked too suspicious. I was terrified of a jail sentence."

Angela stared at Helena a moment longer, then turned and walked off into the house. The question she hadn't asked hung in the air. Were you sleeping with my husband? There it is, thought Helena, why don't you say it? Everyone one else has assumed it for seven years. But murder? How could you think I would help him with murder?

She wheeled herself into the kitchen and turned into the butler's pantry where a dumbwaiter shaft had been converted into an elevator. She was angry and sad – she supposed distraught was the word. Her thoughts were jumbled as she got off on the second floor and went toward her room. Suddenly, one thought came clear. *Cullion*, she said to herself. Of course – the little bastard must be in San Francisco. Only he could pull something like this. He's the only one who knew.

Later, as she sat in her room, she had to admit that Brunetti was also a possibility. But why would either of them implicate themselves like that in the letter, putting allegations about themselves in print that had legal ramifications? Still, they were the ones who knew these things. In the end, Mickey Cullion had to be her best bet. Was he really as illiterate as that blackmail note seemed to show? Or was that note the product of a mind more clever than she realized?

CHAPTER 9

Jake had told Cullion he'd come over right after his shift. During the past couple of weeks, he had gone there every few days, setting things up for his score. Sure, he could let him store a few things he needed to get out of the halfway house. No problem. Jake already had some stuff there, and now he'd be bringing over a duffel bag with some clothes inside and a lock on it. Only in the middle of the underwear and stolen towels would be a certain heavy envelope.

He was itching to count what was in it, but finding a safe place was more important right now. He couldn't bring it to the halfway house and expect nobody to see it. And just suppose there was a surprise search for drugs like they pulled from time to time. No, he could wait to look at it, count it, roll in it. Twenty grand was worth waiting for.

At the mission, he turned into the alley and climbed the outside stairs. The door was open.

"Hi Mike," he said, walking in.

"Good to see you pal. What's that?"

"Duffel bag. I told you I wanted to leave it here, remember?"

"Yeah, sure, go put it in the closet."

Jake could see Cullion had take-out for them, all set up on the little maple table by the room's one window over the alleyway. Playin' house again, he thought. This crap was getting hard to take. Still, he was hungry after his shift.

"Smells like Chinese," he said, looking towards the table.

"You got it, Jake. C'mon, sit down."

He opened the closet and tossed the bag onto the shelf

above the clothes pole, pushing it to the left as far as it would go. Then he shut the door and walked over to the table.

"Whatcha got?" he asked

"Moo-shu pork for you. Chicken lo mein for me."

"Aw-right!"

Jake got settled in and tore into the meal.

Cullion pointed at him with a quizzical look.

"Hey, you shaved off the face fuzz."

"Yeah, gonna start all over. Just a goatee an' mustache this time."

"Looks good to me now."

They were silent for a while as they concentrated on the take-out.

"Listen Jake, how 'bout the job?" Cullion asked. "You goin' full-time soon?"

"Boss says I start next Monday. Forty hours. Got a catch, though. I work Monday thru Thursday, then off two days, then all day Sunday, for Crissake."

"But you can leave the halfway house, right?"

"Well, I got to show a full-time paycheck first, so it'll take a week. Besides, I'll believe it next Monday when my timecard says 'full-time'."

"You can move in here as soon as you're ready."

"I dunno, Mike. One room, you know? It's awful small."

"We can look for a bigger place, and I can get somebody to take this. With two paychecks we could handle it."

Jake grunted and let the moment pass. He hated all that 'we' stuff. Cullion was staring at him hopefully, but he wasn't going to tell him what he wanted to hear. He could only take so much. Tonight he was going to have to stay until ten-thirty, then leave to make his curfew at eleven. And that meant getting cozy – 'ol Mickey wasn't going to be talked into no movie tonight, he could tell. Well, it won't be for much longer, he thought. Jake was already looking for a place he could afford on his own.

CHAPTER 10

When Helena got up Friday morning, she decided not to go downstairs for breakfast with the family. As a result, she knew Angela would assume she was sulking. Well, that's how predictable *she* was. But Helena was more practical than that, and determined.

Determination was always her long suit. Yes, her personality was volatile – no one had to tell her that could be a problem. But she could focus and stay on course with the best of them when it was necessary. And today was one of those times. If Cullion were at the bottom of this, she was going to ferret him out of whatever hole he had found to hide in.

In the middle of Helena's tense reverie, the housekeeper came to check on her. Angela's doing, no doubt. It was eight-thirty.

"May I bring you breakfast, Mrs. Swann?"

Helena managed to smile. "Just orange juice and bran flakes, Esther."

"Is everything all right?"

"Yes, everything is fine. I have phone calls to make and some e-mail correspondence to take care of. I'm not sure whether I'll be down for lunch or not."

"Yes, ma'am. I'll check with you later."

"Oh, Esther? Tell Justin he may stop by during his break if he wants to."

For now, she sat up in bed and tried to concentrate. Mickey Cullion may have been released by now, she thought, but he could be on probation still. When the police found him in 1999, he was in Idaho. Would he have gone back there? One way or the other, he was released in California, so his first parole officer would be here. That would be a start, a way to begin looking for him.

In a few minutes, she remembered the name of someone who could help. Alfonso Bowers. He was the San Francisco police detective who ran the investigation and took her statement after Sam Porter ran off. She recalled his courtesy and his offer of help from the police if she should ever need it. That surely meant official assistance on a police matter, but even so ... she'd think of a way to enlist him to her cause.

Helena plucked her cell phone from the bedside table and scrolled through the emergency numbers she had programmed. After connecting to the police, she heard the typical series of useless menus, choices and announcements, the twenty-first century version of the bureaucratic runaround. Finally, she reached a bored male voice in the Investigations Bureau and asked to speak to Detective Sergeant Alfonso Bowers.

"That's Lieutenant Bowers, ma'am. He's Homicide. I'll forward you, but you'll probably get his voice mail."

"Sure, " she sighed. "Why not?"

~ ~ ~

When he called back later, it was evident that Bowers didn't want her poking around into the old case.

"Lieutenant, I'd like to know something for my piece of mind. Can you tell me whether Mickey Cullion is still in prison?"

"As I recall, Mrs. Swann, he was released in 2001, towards the end of the year."

"Would you put me in touch with the parole officer of record?"

A chilly silence followed before he continued.

"Is there something wrong, Ma'am? May I ask what's bothering you?"

"Well, if I knew where he was located, it might help. For instance, knowing that he went back to Idaho and stayed there would make me feel better."

"But why the concern right now? It's been ... lessee ... eight years since we closed the case and nearly six years since he was paroled."

"Lieutenant, I couldn't have known when he was paroled."

"I suppose not, but it happened a long time ago, and I have this feeling there's something more you could tell me. Is there?"

Helena tried to think fast. It was obvious Bowers didn't want to nose around and locate a private citizen, one who had paid his debt, if he didn't have a legitimate reason. She could go to Brad, whose clout could be applied at the Police Commission, or she could tell Bowers just enough to enlist his sympathy and assistance. Not a real choice, she thought.

"This is probably just a crank thing, Lieutenant, so I didn't want to make an issue of it. I received a letter with some ... accusations. My sister has seen it, too. We're not willing to make it an official police matter. As a matter of fact, neither my brother-in-law nor my sister knows I'm making this call. I just remembered how kind you were to me and thought I might eliminate one cause for concern. As I said, it's probably just a crank letter anyway. We've certainly had others over the years."

"I understand, Mrs. Swann. Maybe I can help you." He sounded much less wary now. "Let me call the parole boys and see what I can find out. In the meantime, don't worry about it. Most likely it's a crank, like you said. One thing, though? If you receive another letter ... you've got to come forward. All right?"

"Yes, Lieutenant. And thank you."

She was surprised when Bowers got back to her the same day. He downplayed the idea that Michael Cullion was the cause of her problem. The guy had an exemplary prison record and went back to Idaho soon after his release. His parole ended in 2005. Apparently, he worked at menial jobs there and had close contact with a local church group.

"So he's still in Idaho?" she asked.

"Well, no. But first I wanted you to know about his record. The parole officer up there was very positive about the guy. He told me Cullion left town to become a kind of assistant to a respected clergyman."

"Oh. Can you tell me where he is?"

"Well, I will, Mrs. Swann. But if I'm ever asked, I'll deny it. I have no reason to follow up on this guy. He's absolutely clean right now."

"Honestly, Lieutenant, I'm glad to hear that."

"Michael Cullion – I'm told he won't respond to Mickey anymore – runs a little storefront church here in San Francisco. They call it the Breastplate of Faith and Love. It's in the Mission district. Entirely legit and respectable, I hear."

~ ~ ~

In retrospect, she should not have called him so soon after speaking to Bowers. A little more time and mental distance might have helped. But a sense of rage led her to search out the mission's telephone number right away. She had gotten out of bed and over to her desk, where she found the number in the white pages. She picked up the landline extension there and punched in the number. When Cullion answered, she lit into him. He didn't respond well to the sarcasm and anger in her voice, and he let her know it.

"Blackmail! What are you talking about, lady?"

"As if you didn't know! You're talking to me, Mickey, remember? I know what you're capable of."

"My name is Michael, Michael Cullion," he said with a certain dignity. "And if you think back, maybe you'll remember some of your own *capabilities* – the words that come to mind are some of the worst ones I know."

He had struck home, and she felt it. But before she had a chance to erupt, he attempted to placate her.

"Listen, this won't do any good. Why don't we both ease off and go to the cops with that letter. I'm not hiding anything."

But that was crazy, she thought. The letter says he's an accessory to murder. Unless ... unless he *doesn't* know about it. And when she probed about the money – he was totally baffled.

Was it Brunetti after all? How could it be? If it were, he wouldn't have accused himself of blackmailing Angela in the letter. Something was going on here; there was someone else in the mix. Someone they hadn't considered or didn't know about.

She wasn't willing to go to the police, of course, but perhaps she could meet with Cullion and talk. If she saw him face to face, she'd be better able to judge him and his motives. But where? She could hardly have him over for drinks.

"You're right, we should figure this out," she said. "But before we get the police involved, I'd like to meet with you."

"I don't know. We never seem to ... communicate real well."

"Look, I shouldn't have said those things. But I believe you'll understand my reaction after seeing this letter."

He paused before responding.

"Well, I work at a diner on Market Street. We could meet there most any day."

He had probably forgotten she was crippled.

"Not too good. My car is equipped for me to drive, but if the diner isn't accessible... "

"Oh, sorry. I suppose I could leave work for an hour or

so some day."

"How about the Palace of Fine Arts tomorrow? I can do that."

He agreed and they settled on meeting the next day, Saturday, at noon.

~ ~ ~

For the short drive to the Palace of Fine Arts, Helena left the motorized scooter behind and took a lightweight chair along that wasn't difficult to fold and store on the passenger side of her car. If she got tired, Cullion could wheel her around. Cruising past the Palace grounds, she spied him sitting on the lawn, silhouetted against the classical rotunda. It was a sunny Saturday, and the park was full of area residents and tourists. The complex was part of the Presidio and bordered on the Marina district. Whenever she came here, Helena recalled a scene from the movie *Vertigo* – Jimmy Stewart and Kim Novak strolling the walkways near the pond.

She finagled the chair out of the car, shifted herself into it, and pushed herself along until she found Cullion, who saw her and nodded. He's changed, she thought. He moves differently now – the fidgety look he used to have is gone. He rose from the grass, brushing his chino slacks off while advancing towards her. Without blinking, he held her gaze.

"I like it here," he said.

"I used to come here often," she said. "But that was a long time ago. I don't get out much any more."

Cullion didn't reply. Instead, he got behind her and began to push the chair along the walk. They both remained silent for a time. When she saw a likely spot on the lawn near the pond's edge, she pointed and he wheeled her onto the grass and down, reaching level ground near some bushes within sight of the swans. There was no one within thirty feet of them.

"We've never had much use for each other, have we?" she said, smiling.

"I know I've had my reasons, Mrs. Swann."

"When all is said and done, though, Sam Porter was the problem – not you and I."

"Maybe so. But this isn't about him, is it?"

"In a way it is. Judge for yourself."

Helena pulled a copy of the letter from her purse, unfolded it, and handed it to Cullion. He took it, looked at her blankly, and sat on the ground by the side of her chair. As he read, she saw the anger and hurt play on his features. First Angela, then she, and now Michael Cullion – all three of them had the same smoldering reaction. When he handed the letter back to her, she spoke.

"Could this be Brunetti's work? Would he do something like this?"

"Nah. Nobody is less likely than Pedro Brunetti to give the law a chance to nail him."

"My thought exactly," she said.

He laughed. "But you thought I would?"

"Sorry. I did think it was you until we spoke."

"Y' know, I don't know how to say this," he started. "Sometimes you just gotta talk to somebody. There was an old guy helped me in prison ... a preacher. I told him this stuff, I needed to. But he would never have done this. He's dead now, anyhow. And there was someone else I trusted, too ... until now."

"Then you know who did this? Do you?"

Cullion sighed. "'Fraid so. Did she give him the twenty grand like he asked?"

"No. Just ten."

He got to his feet and began wheeling her back to the walk. She twisted around in the chair to look up at him.

"Can we do something about this?" she asked.

"Oh, I'm gonna to take care of it," he said. "There

won't be any follow up letters. I can't promise I'll get the money back, but I'll try. Can we keep the cops out of it?"

"The last thing we want is police involvement or anything that will cause publicity."

"Good. Then give me a chance to make it right."

~ ~ ~

Helena hadn't spoken to her sister since their awful blowup. Poor Angela was distancing herself at the very moment she needed help and solace from someone. After doing what she could to mitigate any further blackmail attempt, she had to be in dread of what would come next. When Helena saw her late that afternoon, she hoped to ease her mind.

At first their talk was strained. Then Helena brought the conversation around to Justin – his lessons and after school activities.

"You know, the last thing I ever expected was to be a soccer mom," Angela said. "But as it turns out, I love it."

"Who'd a thunk it?" laughed Helena.

Although Angela managed a smile, it was fleeting. "I haven't wanted to talk about this, Helena, because the whole subject is stressful for me, but I'm sorry for the accusation I made. I know you weren't involved in Wanda Buckley's murder."

Helena was stunned, but grateful. "It hurt me, you know, hearing you say that. But when I thought about it … well, I could understand why you doubted me."

An awkward silence intervened. She wondered how best to let Angela know what she had done since yesterday. Finally, she forced herself to speak about her conversations with Lieutenant Bowers and Mickey Cullion. Angela's hands fluttered to her face as she listened to the rush of words. There was fear in her eyes when Helena described her meeting with Mickey.

"Oh, was that wise, dear?" she asked.

"I was angry and I had to find out. I felt I was under a cloud. And I'm glad I confronted him, Angela. Mickey wants to set things right. He knows who's behind this and he's going to keep the blackmailer quiet."

"Did you find out who it is? His name, I mean?"

"No. I wanted to ask, but suddenly I thought it better not to know."

CHAPTER 11

The whole Michael Cullion thing is over, he thought. He was just plain ol' Mickey again, the low life thief who gets led down the friggin' garden path by some good-looking creep. How had it come to this? If his knowledge of the human heart had grown under Jim Hendrickson's tutelage, why hadn't his resistance to its weakness grown as well? Standing in front of the dresser mirror, he stared hard at himself. He was thirty-nine years old and felt every day of it. People told him he looked much younger, but that was his size: a little guy always seems younger than his years.

He knew what to do to make this right, he thought, but where would he go from there? The thing with Julie was over, he had messed that up for sure. And the whole fantasy he had built up around Jake? Just another self-delusion, he knew, one he seemed fated to repeat over and over. Well, it stops here, he said to himself. He had spent his whole life so far trying to prove himself and his good intentions to other people. *From now on, let them prove themselves to me!*

He found himself fiddling about in the dresser's top drawer, looking in at the socks and underwear neatly folded and stored there. Putting one hand underneath the stacks of clothing, he slid it along from right to left at the bottom of the drawer until he felt the resistance of a small box. Then he raised the box lid and stared for a long time at the articles inside.

Suddenly, he remembered the duffel bag. He had completely forgotten that Jake had asked to store it. Opening the closet door, Cullion spotted the olive drab bag with the zipper lock on the shelf to the far left. He pulled it down to look. The lock would be easy to break, but he couldn't bring himself to do it. After all, he should let the guy defend himself first. But it wouldn't hurt to heft it and try to feel what was inside.

The bag was chock full of clothes and try as he might, he couldn't feel anything else through the rough cloth exterior. Ah, who knows, he thought. He'd just have to wait for Jake to show up. Man, he'd like to give him the benefit of the doubt, but everything pointed to betrayal and a complete lack of scruples. What had he done to deserve this?

~ ~ ~

On Friday, Jake Snider had to sweat it out at the halfway house. He figured he might as well stay around in case the cops came calling. Not that he expected trouble, but if they were looking for him – well, here he would be, not hiding, not worried, and nothing to be found on the premises. Whenever he got too antsy, he would think about all that long, cool, green stuff in the duffel bag at Cullion's place.

After his shift on Thursday, he had gone to his locker, buried the envelope in the duffel bag, and left the building. Once on the street, he went around to the service entrance and retrieved the windbreaker, sunglasses, and baseball cap, sticking them inside his jacket. A few blocks away, he broke the glasses and threw the two halves into different trash receptacles. In similar fashion, he ripped the ponytail out of the hat, throwing each part away in separate trash bins on his way to Cullion's place. The windbreaker was thin enough to fold small and leave in his inside pocket – until he returned to the house and hung it up where he had found it.

If no one had seen him go into that service entrance after he took the package from Angela Styles, he could not be traced. No way. And he didn't think he had been spotted. Still, he couldn't help but go over every single detail of what happened: from the charity ball – to the drop off – to Thursday night with Cullion. By nightfall, he felt pretty good. More than twenty-four hours had passed and there was no newspaper story, no cops, no problem. He could even concentrate on the *Las Vegas* episode he was watching with the other guys in the common room.

Around two o'clock on Saturday, Jake was walking past the Breastplate of Faith and Love Mission, heading for the alley. He had keys to the back entrance now, and he figured on getting the duffel bag down from the closet shelf to check out his score. If Cullion wasn't around, that is. If he was – well, he might have to wait until Monday. Despite what he had told him, he already had permission to leave the halfway house, and Monday would be the day he took all his shit over to the new place he found just this morning. Yeah ... no more Mission, no more Mickey, no more 'we.'

~ ~ ~

Cullion watched the back door open and stared at Jake when he walked in. He was sitting on his bed and trying to think what he wanted to say. But no words came, and by now Jake was staring back with a funny look on his face.

Jake said: "Hey, what's up? What's going on?"

"I gotta know something, Jake. I get the feeling lately I don't mean a damn thing to you. Is that right?"

"Whoa, Mike. You know I don't talk about stuff like that. Can it, man."

"Oh ... you know what, Jake? You don't have to bother with Mike and Michael any more, it's just Mickey like it used to be. Nothing ever changes, huh?"

"What the fuck is this? You got some big dramatic scene in mind, play it yourself! I'm not havin' any!"

"Well, what are you havin', Jake? Some blackmail maybe? Some score, some profit from things I talked about?"

Jake was quiet a moment. Cullion could practically see him trying to figure out what had happened. He almost felt sorry for him.

"Ten grand is chump change, Jake. I can't believe you took all that risk for ten grand!"

Jake's mouth dropped open and his eyes started. He leapt to the closet door, tearing it open and flinging the duffel bag over to the bed. Quickly, he had his keys out, got the lock off, and was digging the underwear and towels out of the bag to get at the envelope. Cullion looked on sadly and shook his head.

When Jake opened the package, you could see the stacks of bills had been augmented with newspaper to fill out the envelope. There was a note inside as well. Cullion watched anger darken the big man's eyes and twist his features as he read it. Finally, Jake jammed everything back into the bag, kicked it into the open closet, and slammed the door shut.

"C'mon Jake. Forget it, you know? Ten grand ain't worth it. We can make it right, see? We can still make things work. Give it back and they'll never come after you. They don't want anybody to know!"

"Fuck! Ten lousy grand! That cunt!"

Jake had grabbed Cullion by the shirtfront and was shaking him. His lips were pulled back from his teeth, and his nostrils flared.

"How the fuck did you know there's ten grand in there?"

"Give the money back, Jake," Cullion pleaded. "I know we could still make it work!"

"Always with the goddamn '*we*' shit!" he yelled. "It was never '*we*,' you little asshole!"

Jake slapped him hard across the face with one hand. He pushed him backwards and knelt on his arms, pinning him to the floor. Cullion felt his nose break and his teeth loosen under the quick, sharp blows. Desperate, he used the limited freedom of his right arm to reach into his trouser pocket and take out the knife he had gotten from the dresser drawer. The knife he had put away for good so long ago.

Cullion flicked the button, jerked free his arm, and aimed true, right under the breastbone. He sliced, twisted, and pushed until he could feel his hand start to slide in with the blade.

Suddenly, Jake jumped back. His hands flew in surprise to his open belly as he fell on the bed. Cullion sat up on the floor and watched, covered in blood from his broken nose. Jake yelled out – loud – but it became a scream, the pitch going high and weird, then trailing off as he ran out of breath.

When another scream filled the silence, Cullion turned his battered face to see the young immigrant couple who rented the apartment. They were standing in the doorway of his room, horror masks for faces.

CHAPTER 12

When Detective Maynard Bennett took the call, he couldn't quite believe his ears. He had never heard of the victim, Jake Snider, but the name Michael Lester Cullion was all too familiar from the old Porkpie case. With his then partner Al Bowers, Bennett had investigated Wanda Buckley's murder eight years ago. They had subsequently taken it on the chin when Sam Porter eluded capture in San Francisco. The public was not pleased, and the Police Commission had a meltdown. Despite having his throat cut by Porter, Cullion also got out of town before they could apprehend him. Sure, he was finally tracked down and did time, but it was a Las Vegas detective who found him up there in Idaho. In short, the Porkpie case had been nothing but humiliation and misery for San Francisco homicide.

The first phase of the Snider investigation was quick, clean, and easy. Cullion was Mirandized and immediately confessed. And it was all videotaped. Now, some lawyer was bound to come along and try to have it thrown out, but that was just part of today's legal playscript. A professional like Bennett wasn't going to worry about stuff he couldn't control. For the present, everything was in order.

Except that he wasn't satisfied Cullion had given him a full picture. The murder had all the earmarks of the classic 'homo-cide,' but Cullion wasn't owning up to a sexual relationship. They had an argument, he admitted, but it was about some unspecified wrong Snider had done to a third party. Cullion wouldn't say more because he didn't want to involve an innocent person. He did what he had to do in self-defense, he said. So, what Bennett had on record was Cullion's detailed description of the actual fight and murder, which matched the physical aspects of the scene perfectly. It was certainly enough for now.

Juan and Margarita Cansillo were on record also. Juan had called the police at Cullion's request. He and his wife had seen the immediate aftermath of the murder, and everything they said coincided with Cullion's confession. If he couldn't claim "case closed," Bennett was nevertheless happy to give his initial report to Al Bowers, who was his boss now.

Happy, that is, until the crime scene techs handed in the list of evidence found at the scene. And happy until Bowers came charging into the squad room with a real mystified look on his face. Now Bowers wasn't miffed at the list of evidence, even though it included a bombshell – the duffel bag with ten grand in it. He seemed to focus on the third party angle instead.

"Why the hell," he wanted to know, "haven't you found out Cullion's motive in more concrete terms, and who he's protecting?"

"Hey, Boss, this is day one of the investigation. Cut me some freakin' slack! I've got a confession, and it coincides with the known evidence. What more could you want in the first twenty-four hours?"

Now he had to agree with Bowers that the ten grand and the underlying reason for the fight were related. It sure didn't take a lot of brainpower to put that together. Cullion had shrugged it off however, telling them he didn't know where the money came from. He claimed that Snider stored the bag in his closet, but that he, Cullion, had never looked inside. At that point he lawyered up, just like that.

"Okay," Bowers said. "When a public defender is appointed, let me know. We have enough for arraignment Monday anyway. That'll keep the brass happy for now. What about the press? Anybody sniff this one out yet?"

"So far it just smells like Mission district mayhem and murder, unless some old hand recognizes Cullion's name."

"That'll happen in no time, May."

"Yeah, I suppose you're right."

"Let's give some thought to that before I call the chief. I'd like to give him some suggestions for the public relations angle."

Bennett asked himself what the hell that was about. Why should he worry about the public relations department? That wasn't like Al Bowers at all.

"Oh, one thing more, May. Was there anything else in that duffel bag that could relate to this?"

"No. Just ... um ... towels, underwear, the money, some newspaper, and a large envelope. The money, newspaper, and envelope were kind of pushed in there, on top. The bag was locked when they found it, and the keys were in Snider's pocket."

"Were the Cansillos asked about the bag?"

"They were, yes. They never saw it. They couldn't be sure about the closet being closed, although they thought it was. Of course, they did leave Cullion in the room by himself when he asked them to call the police."

~ ~ ~

Angela Styles was at breakfast Tuesday morning when she first saw the headline. Setting her coffee down, she felt confused and sickish all at once.

PORKPIE ACCOMPLICE SUSPECTED
IN SNIDER SLAYING
MICKEY 'WEASEL' CULLION IN CUSTODY

She read all their names in the first column under the banner – hers, Helena's, and Brad's – although there was nothing in the story to link them to this new atrocity. They were only mentioned in reference to the old scandal, thank God. And there was nothing about money! Even though

145

Cullion had confessed to the murder – disembowelment was the awful term they used – the only reason he gave was self-defense. There had been an argument of some kind, followed by their fight. The photo of the arraignment showed that he had taken a terrible beating. Was it possible all this had nothing to do with the blackmail attempt?

Unless ... unless Helena had done something, paid money perhaps to Cullion to ... get rid of the blackmailer! *Oh God, please no*, she thought.

When Brad came downstairs, he was dressed for work and ready to leave.

"Don't go just yet, dear," she said. "Please stay to breakfast."

"What's the matter, Angela?" He stood there frowning.

She raised her eyebrows and handed him the newspaper. When he had scanned the headline and read the first paragraph, he stopped and looked at her.

"I can't believe it," he said. "Has Helena seen this yet?" he asked.

"She hasn't been down. Read the whole article, Brad."

When he had, she could see him relax a little.

"Well, I guess that could have been worse," he said.

"So far, yes. But, darling ... I've something to tell you."

Brad's face was tense and flushed, but he listened quietly. She told him about the charity ball, the waiter, the delivery of the money. After describing her angry scene with Helena, she pulled the blackmail note from her robe and gave it to him.

He sat down next to her at the kitchen island. Slowly, he read the note.

"Angela," he sighed, "this is awful, but I don't see any connection between the murder in the newspaper and this ... thing."

"I know. But Helena found out Cullion was in town.

And she met with him on Saturday. He figured out who was blackmailing me, and he agreed to make sure it would stop."

Brad looked at her, baffled. She hesitated before speaking again.

"I ... can't help but wonder if she could have paid him to ... get rid of this man. Perhaps Snider was the blackmailer."

"Paid Cullion?" he asked. "To kill somebody? There was a time when I would have been quick to defend her against such a terrible accusation. But after everything that's happened ...."

"Well, I couldn't help wondering, but that doesn't make it true. Maybe we should just wait, Brad. We have no reason to accuse her of anything."

"I suppose you're right. That's just what we'll do. Why ask for trouble?"

After a minute, Brad spoke again.

"I'm worried about you, Angela. Why didn't you come to me? What could you have been thinking?" His face told her he was devastated.

She tried to blink back the tears. "Oh, honey, after everything you've been through with Helena and me, I wanted to protect you for once. I thought I could take care of it."

Brad stayed home with her until late morning.

~ ~ ~

Maynard Bennett had made a routine request for phone records and was looking through a list of incoming calls for the Breastplate of Faith and Love Mission. The physical telephone was a landline in Cullion's room. One number on the report stood out – and it belonged to Mr. And Mrs. Bradford Styles. Ohmigod, thought Bennett, this can't be happening. The last thing he ever expected in this case was a new link between Cullion and those people.

The call had come in at 4:35 PM on Friday, the day before the murder. Right away, Bennett left a message for Al Bowers and one with Angela Styles's housekeeper. Mrs. Styles was the first to call back.

"What can I do for you, Detective?" she asked.

"Mrs. Styles, I'm sorry to disturb you. By now I'm sure you've seen the stories on the Cullion case, and I want you to know we think it's a shame the press has chosen to dredge up the old news."

"Yes, I've seen them. And thank you, but I suppose it was inevitable."

"One small thing has come up that I hope you can help me with."

"Oh?"

"Yes, a telephone call from your landline came in to the Breastplate of Faith and Love Mission last Friday. A three-minute phone call. Can you shed any light on this?"

"No, I can't. Are you sure about this, Detective?"

"Yes. I double-checked before calling you."

"Well, I had several guests on Friday. And there are the household members ... and Esther, my employee. But I can't imagine anyone calling there. That's Culllion's church, isn't it?"

"That's right."

"Well, I don't see how I can help you."

"If you would, ma'am, you could do just two things for us. Ask the members of your household about this. Someone might recall something. And help me make a list of everybody who was a guest at your house Friday."

"Detective, if there was a phone call from my home to that place, it *had* to be a mistake, some kind of misdial perhaps."

"I see what you're saying, Mrs. Styles. But it's something I need to follow through on. Could you help me put that list together, Ma'am? It couldn't take long."

He knew he had handled this call as well or better than anyone else could have. But she wasn't having any.

"I'm sorry. I don't think I want to do that. No offense, Detective Bennett, but I think this request should be put in writing to my lawyer. I'm sure you remember him. He had to intervene the last time, when I thought some police requests were intrusive. Please don't take this personally. You've been most polite. But I can't help you."

Checkmate, he said to himself. With her connections in the judiciary and among the very highest city brass, it would be months before they had a list. He knew it was still his case, but Al Bowers would have to take over the high society aspect. Good luck to him.

And now, he wondered, what was Cullion going to say about that phone call?

CHAPTER 13

Lieutenant Alfonso Bowers was proud of his career in the SFPD. When he was a kid, he thought he would become an army drill instructor like his dad. Somewhere along the way his fascination for military life wore off, but all the lessons he had absorbed on discipline and team building pushed him into law enforcement. And it suited him. He loved investigative work, despite the politics and social pressures you ran up against in a city like San Francisco.

So here he was, a middle-aged black man, a respected figure on the San Francisco police force, devoted husband and father to three kids – and, since last Friday, a guy with a problem. When he helped Helena Swann find Cullion, he did it out of respect – she had been very cooperative back in the day, during the Porkpie investigation in 1999. But he should never have done it. He hoped it wouldn't prove to be a case of – what was the saying? ... *no good deed ever goes unpunished.*

He felt sorry for Helena Swann; he saw her as ill-used. From his point of view, it was bizarre to think of her as the Black Widow while Mrs. Styles was Saint Angela to all and sundry. The heroism that Angela had showed in sticking by her husband, a vicious killer, was simply obstruction of justice to a policeman. However, he had to wonder if Mrs. Swann had manipulated him into a corner this time around. Well, he'd have to straighten that out.

When Bennett came to him about the telephone call from the Styles residence to the Breastplate of Faith and Love, he was only too happy to take over that aspect of the investigation. Later in the day, they met to go over all of the evidence. There was a ton, and it all pointed in one direction. Mickey Cullion was going down, in spades.

"How did the arraignment go?" he asked Bennett.

"Held without bail, like we wanted. Judge Shafter barely listened to the public defender before making the decision."

"Great. Although I wouldn't want to be up on charges before a judge named Shafter," he chuckled.

Bennett seldom laughed at his jokes. This one was no exception.

"His lawyer entered the not guilty plea, like we figured, while Cullion stood there shaking his head."

"When you talked to him last time, what did Cullion say about the phone call?"

"He said he never got a phone call on Friday."

"Damn. Did you show him the list of calls?"

"Nah. I just asked if he got any calls. And I asked if he were sure when he said no. I handled it like you said."

"And the public defender?"

"She didn't pick up on it at all. You were right about that, too."

"Good, May, good. I want to keep the phone call quiet for now. Especially, I don't want anything in the news – but I don't want his lawyer in on it either. Not just yet, anyway."

"But Al, the discovery period? The defense?"

"If we find out it's exculpatory or even neutral, we'll give it to them, of course. For right now it's my decision that it's meaningless. If it remains that way, we'll *still* give it to them. But not while Cullion won't talk and we're still investigating."

"And the ten grand?"

"Keep it out of the press. As long as the defense doesn't know about the phone call, it's in their best interest to keep quiet about the money."

"Well, you're checking the phone call now, so fine with me. But how am I supposed to keep on investigating the money? I have no where to go with it."

"Hey ... don't give up May. Shit, think about it!"

"Yeah, sure Al," he groaned. "Who are you going to see about the phone call?"

"Well, Mrs. Styles can't stop me from interviewing anyone who wants to talk. And I'm quite sure Helena Swann will see me. She's a household member who could have made the call. Right?"

"Interesting choice."

"Isn't it, though? And I see no reason not to ask her why she thinks Mickey Cullion had ten thousand bucks in his closet."

"You gotta be kidding, Al."

"Not at all. I just told you the money is still under investigation, didn't I?"

~ ~ ~

He was standing in Helena Swann's bedroom – boudoir, he supposed he should call it – which was nearly the size of his whole apartment in Pacific Heights. Which made it what – fifteen hundred square feet? Damn big anyway. He glanced up at the twelve-foot-high coffered ceiling. The crown molding and the waist-high paneling surrounding the room were finely crafted from gleaming walnut. Above the paneling, the walls were covered in a deep pink watered silk.

Lord, what a lot to take in. There were two double-door entrances to the room, both of them featuring a kind of bull's eye mirror ensconced in an elaborate half-round transom panel above the fluted walnut doorframes. Drapery, chair fabrics and carpets in the room tended toward yellows and greens, except for the backdrop to the bed's canopy, which was a pleated material in royal blue.

The bed itself was relatively small, no larger than full-size, which he thought might relate to her disability somehow. He certainly couldn't tell antiques from reproductions, but he had no doubt the quality of each piece of furniture was high. The bed, chests, and dressers were made of crotch mahogany; other pieces appeared to be either walnut or tiger maple. The tabletops had the beautiful patterns and striations of fine veneers.

Well, he had expected to be impressed. When he arranged the meeting, he wondered if Angela and Brad Styles would be there as well. From the peremptory way Mrs. Styles had treated Bennett, that would have been tantamount to letting him know his visit was futile. But Mrs. Swann had suggested a time when the Styleses would be out of the house. They would have the place nearly to themselves, she said. Except, of course, for Justin Styles and his tutor ... and the housekeeper, who had just announced him.

After greeting him, Helena Swann shifted herself from the motorized scooter into an armless easy chair, then gestured to a loveseat covered in pearl white damask. He sat down, adjusting his trousers to preserve the crease. She watched as he did this and smiled approvingly. The type of person, he thought, who notices every nuance of body language and assigns a value to it.

Bowers could see the opening gambit would be his. She would sit there serenely until he committed himself. If this were going to be a game of cat and mouse, he had no doubt she intended to be the cat.

"Your suite is lovely, Mrs. Swann. Words fail me," he said.

"I spend so much time here, I'm afraid I fuss over it a great deal."

"The result is ... beyond charming. It's perfect."

"How nice of you to say that!"

He couldn't think of a good transition, so he waded in.

"Mrs. Swann, when you called me last week about Mickey Cullion ..."

She interrupted. "But Lieutenant, we both know that never happened. Remember what you said?"

Whoa, he thought, she wants to hold that over me and take control of the interview.

"I said I'd deny telling you where Cullion was. For now we can let that lie, Mrs. Swann. But denial won't work if it bumps up against my responsibilities. I'm sure you understand."

He had made her stop and think.

"Yes, perhaps I do," she said. "As you see it, where does that leave us?"

"I'm only interested in your honest responses to three questions, ma'am."

"I see. What are they?"

"When you called me, you mentioned a letter you received that contained certain accusations. May I see it?"

"I'm sorry, Lieutenant Bowers, but I told you I wasn't willing to turn that into a police matter."

"What were the accusations?"

"Just the ravings of a crank. I won't talk about this any further."

Bowers sighed.

"My second question is about a phone call." He placed the report on the table between them and pointed to the entry with Brad and Angela's landline number. "Did you make this call to the Breastplate of Faith and Love Mission last Friday, Mrs. Swann?"

"I did not."

"I see," he nodded. "Let me put that another way. Did you make this call to Michael Cullion about an hour after we spoke last Friday?"

This time she hesitated before smiling and responding.

"If I'm not mistaken, a Detective Bennett spoke to my sister about that phone call. I think you should follow her advice and contact her lawyer about it."

He knew he was glowering now; he couldn't help it. She had no intention to be forthcoming. But he needed to press on.

"Well then, on to my final question. What do you know about a large sum of money found in Cullion's possession?"

She remained cool, but her eyes told him the question startled her. Why would that be? She either knew about the money or she didn't. Which was it?

"Absolutely nothing. How much did he have?"

He decided to ignore her question and wait for a further reaction. It wasn't long in coming.

"Lieutenant, you've asked your three questions. May I show you out? I'm sure we both have a lot to do this afternoon."

Again he ignored her. "I wonder," he said.

"You wonder ... ?"

"I wonder if Jake Snider did something to make you pay Mickey Cullion to get rid of him for you."

"How dare you accuse me of such a thing!"

"Ah, Mrs. Swann, I'm afraid you misunderstand me," he said, rising to go. "I accuse no one, I was just wondering."

He had spoken softly, with a smile. And he forced himself to remain smiling as he left. On the stairway to the first floor, he saw a young boy staring at him. This must be Angela Styles's son, he thought, the child she had by Sam Porter.

~ ~ ~

It might not have been wise to telegraph his suspicions and the direction of his investigation to Helena Swann. But with both sisters stonewalling, he needed to shake things up. And the shake up wouldn't stop there, he thought.

At headquarters, he called in his friend Bennett and told him he was taking over as lead investigator. You didn't often catch May Bennett showing his anger, but he let him have it this time.

"You bigfooting me, Al? What the fuck for?"

"Whoa, May, easy! It's the Sharples family. The phone call and the money point their way. You gave them to me, remember?"

"Yeah, I remember all right. I also remember I'm the guy who took Cullion's confession, for Crissake! We already have the murderer and the evidence to convict him, and that was on my watch!"

"Look, you know you're not satisfied with Cullion's story. If the defense had the phone call as well as the money right now, they'd be making hay in the press and we'd never get Angela Styles or Helena Swann to loosen up."

Bowers didn't blame Bennett for being pissed. He couldn't tell him yet, but part of his motivation was selfish – protecting his own ass from the mistake of helping Helena Swann to begin with. He'd make sure to tie Bennett in to the next grueling step he had to take: a meeting with the police chief and the president of the Police Commission.

There was nothing in the world he dreaded more than calling those two together to discuss an investigation they assumed to be closed. The chief, Dan Cinzano, was a career cop who would understand where he was coming from. Bowers would approach him first and lay out the problem. Because of the power and influence represented by Sharples Communications, he'd ask the chief to call in Hilary Saunders, president of the Police Commission. Together, the three of them would have to decide how to approach the remaining evidence.

Those were the political realities Bowers had to face;

the problem would be Saunders. In a city of ultra-liberals, she stood out as the most recalcitrant cop-hater of them all. Every use of force was occasion for another blistering attack through the media and another call for investigations and special reporting. The only cop who passed muster with her was the cop who took the social worker approach to police work, thus avoiding pursuit and danger at all costs. And yet, she had the connections that could make things happen in San Francisco. If she would get behind them, folks like Angela Styles and Helena Swann might suddenly open up and begin to cooperate.

The thing that stuck most sharply in his craw was the possibility he would have to admit his error. If it struck her as useful politically, Hilary Saunders might choose to give him a public spanking that would hurt him career-wise and be personally humiliating. No matter how he diced and sliced that one, his ego would take a terrific beating. Well, he thought, set it to rest for now: no use buying trouble in advance.

CHAPTER 14

Chief Cinzano called a meeting for ten o'clock the next morning. For her part, Ms. Saunders insisted they meet at her office; she needed to prepare for a presentation at noon and couldn't leave. Otherwise, they'd have to schedule it another day. Bowers suspected the jockeying had more to do with turf and power issues than any practical consideration. Both officials worked at 850 Bryant Street, so it didn't matter in the least to him whose office he sat in, as long as it happened real soon.

When the four of them gathered in her spaces at ten, Hilary Saunders spent the first five minutes on the phone, discussing audio-visual equipment and the physical set-up for her presentation. When she hung up, she turned to the three men without apology and peered at them over her glasses.

"Well, fellas, what can I do for you today?" she said brightly.

Cinzano introduced Bennett. Saunders and Bowers had already met. The chief went on to explain the circumstances that brought them to her. It was their belief she could smooth the way to a productive meeting with Angela Styles and Helena Swann about the telephone call and the ten thousand dollars.

"Let me get a few things straight first," she said with some asperity. "From the newspaper accounts, I thought Bennett here was in charge, but you're telling me Bowers has taken over. What's that about?"

Bowers spoke up. "It was my judgment, Commissioner, that Detective Bennett had no way to pursue the telephone call or the money evidence after being stonewalled by Mrs. Styles."

"And so you took over and got stonewalled by Helena Swann. Where'd that get us?"

"Hilary," Cinzano interrupted, "the assignment and reassignment of detectives is my concern, not yours. You know that. Let's get on with this."

"Well excuse me, Dan," she said, "but it seems to me Detective Bennett secured the evidence, arrested the suspect and took his confession. Assuming he didn't manufacture the evidence or use coercion to obtain the confession – always a concern with your boys – he should get a commendation. What do *you* say about this, Detective Bennett?"

"What I say, Ms. Saunders, is that you seem more interested in giving us grief than in helping us. Why is that?"

Bowers couldn't believe Maynard Bennett had it in him to fence like that with somebody in power. He glanced over at Cinzano, only to see him looking straight ahead and smirking. After staring coldly at Bennett for a few moments, Hilary Saunders burst out laughing.

"Bravo, Detective Bennett, bravo! But you see, I have to listen to the citizens of San Francisco every day. They complain to me on a depressingly regular basis about the grief given to them by your colleagues on the force. So it's fitting that the grief comes full circle, don't you think?"

Bennett opened his mouth to reply, but Chief Cinzano stepped in.

"No, we're not going to play this game, gentlemen. Hilary is either going to help us ... or not. We can go to the press ourselves right now about the telephone call and the ten thousand dollars, and let them connect the dots to Angela Styles and Helena Swann." He paused then and turned to Saunders with a wide-eyed look. "Oh ... but they're your friends, aren't they, Hilary?"

"Very good, Dan," she said. "Well done. And now that

you've put both your cards and mine on the table, what is it you need from me?"

"We want you to arrange a meeting with Angela and Brad Styles about the phone call to Cullion's church. We think Helena Swann should be there too. You would host the meeting, Bowers and I would attend."

"What about representation from the D.A.'s office?"

"I don't see that you need that. We're just asking a few questions about a three-minute phone call, Hilary."

"What's the reason we want Helena Swann to attend? The phone line isn't in her name."

"No, but she lives with them and she knows Cullion. And we want to see how they react – all of them – to questions about the money."

Saunders pushed back in her chair and crossed her arms.

"No, I don't think so. You told me you have no evidence to link any of these people to that money. I'm not at all sure I want to bring it up. I'll play that one by ear."

"Where does that leave us?" asked Cinzano. He wasn't looking at Saunders any longer, and his jaw was pushed out.

"Helena Swann won't be attending, and no one will ask questions about the money ... unless I do."

It was like pulling teeth, but they had their meeting.

~ ~ ~

Brad Styles reserved the boardroom at Sharples Communications for them. He and Mrs. Styles were there when Bowers and Dan Cinzano arrived. Hilary Saunders arrived late, sweeping into the room with greetings and apologies for her tardiness.

Bowers knew that Ms. Saunders was on the board of directors at Sharples Communications and that she and Angela Styles were board members for the San Francisco Repertory Company, a non-profit theater group. Their social lives and professional lives crisscrossed any number of times a year and in any number of ways. And even though she never said so, Bowers knew she had been a close childhood friend of Helena Swann. He wondered if relations among the elite in other cities were as incestuous as these.

The boardroom was an enormous affair at the top of the Tremont building downtown. It managed to be modern and pompous without having a great deal of distinction. A series of interlocking rosewood sections formed themselves into one giant conference table nearly forty feet long. As many as two-dozen gray leather chairs surrounded the table. The room and its amenities seemed to overwhelm the little party of five.

Brad Styles's administrative assistant served coffee. A silver tray with fresh pastries from a nearby bakery sat on a credenza under the windows. Bowers coveted one of these, but held back when everyone else declined.

At first, Hilary Saunders chatted easily with Brad and Angela Styles, making no effort to bring the chief or Bowers into the conversation. This seemed to embarrass Brad and Angela, who would at least look their way and smile from time to time. Finally, Saunders made sure everyone had been introduced and began to talk about the telephone call.

"Angela, we wanted to question anyone who might have made the call from your house to Cullion's mission, but you objected to making a list of everyone who was in the house that Friday. Is that about right?"

"Yes, I asked Detective Bennett to pursue it with my lawyer."

"All right, I understand. There is a problem you should be aware of, though. The phone call is a piece of evidence to us. While we are still investigating, we can control access to evidence to a certain extent."

"We understand that, Hilary." It was Brad speaking.

"Good, good. You're probably also aware that we sometimes share evidence with the press when we think it will help us ascertain a fuller picture of a crime."

Saunders let that sink in for a moment. Then she continued.

"The other thing that happens with evidence is generally out of our control. When the defense receives evidence as part of the discovery process, they may look at it and think of ways to present it as a smoking gun. And they often leak it, or even just present it outright to the press with a theory that it tends to exonerate their client and point to someone else."

Bowers realized that Hilary Saunders had done a nice job of putting the Styleses on the spot without squeezing them overtly. Angela Styles looked downcast, but Brad smiled and began to chuckle.

"Chief, based on Hilary's scenario here, why don't we rescind that silly demand of ours about the lawyer."

"Of course, Mr. Styles, we'd be happy to have your cooperation."

"Perhaps you won't mind if we personally ask everyone about the phone call before turning a list over to you. That would make it go down a lot easier, I'm sure."

"Certainly, sir."

Everyone was smiling now, even Angela Styles, but Bowers wasn't satisfied. It had gone so well, he knew Saunders would not be inclined to ask about the ten grand. It was time, though, and he had to know.

"There is one other thing to discuss," he said. "When Michael Cullion was apprehended, we found ten thousand dollars in his room."

Hilary Saunders had an angry look on her face and was signaling for him to stop. He was sure Dan Cinzano was horrified, although he just stared. Bowers went on without a pause.

"I'm bringing this up because of a serious lapse in judgment I made a day before the murder. Your sister called me, Mrs. Styles, and asked me to help her locate Michael Cullion. She said she received a threatening letter and she wanted to make sure he wasn't in town. I went ahead and checked, figuring I could allay her concerns. Mrs. Swann wouldn't share the letter, claiming it was probably from a crank. What I found out was that Cullion was running a legitimate church in town. I shouldn't have told her where he was, but I did. And the next day, Cullion killed Jake Snider. In light of all this, the ten thousand dollars loom very large. Where did that money come from?"

"Lieutenant Bowers, surely you don't expect Brad or Angela to know the answer to that question!" Hilary Saunders was livid, and she wasn't making the slightest effort to hide her fury or her contempt.

"No, Ms. Saunders, but I'd like them to reflect on it and get back to me if they think of something that might help."

Screw her, he thought. At least he'd be able to look at himself in the mirror when this was over. If he still had a mirror, that is.

CHAPTER 15

Angela had been devastated by Lieutenant Bowers's revelation at the meeting with Hilary Saunders. So they knew about the money all along, she thought. Yet it was all so confusing. If Jake Snider had been the blackmailer, why did the money wind up in Cullion's room? Did they have an argument over splitting the money, or was Cullion telling the truth when he said the fight was over something Snider had done to a third person – namely, her? As often as she looked at the newspaper articles and the picture they ran of Snider, she couldn't identify him as either of the men she had seen.

And her note – the note she put into the envelope to warn the blackmailer against further contact – why hadn't Bowers mentioned that? If it was gone, who got rid of it? Was Cullion covering up for her? Helena said she told him about the blackmail and the money, and he was supposed to try to get the money back. Was that true?

Or did Helena's involvement go deeper? Could she have encouraged Cullion to kill Snider and keep the money, despite what she said? That might put an entirely different face on what Cullion was doing. Once again, she found herself doubting her sister's reasons for acting as she did.

The salient feature of that blackmail letter, the most damaging allegation that it contained, after all, was that Helena had been an accomplice to a murder committed eight years ago. That was a powerful motive for acting to harm the blackmailer. Brad would have to help her sort this out. She knew he would be supportive, although she wasn't so sure he would give Helena the benefit of the doubt.

Around five o'clock Esther fed Justin and left for the night. Angela took him up to his room then, where they talked about his lessons. He seemed anxious to play computer games, so she didn't linger long. She greeted Brad in the foyer when he got in at six o'clock, and they decided on a quiet supper together. While they sat at the big kitchen island with soft drinks and the burgers she had just grilled, Angela confided her fears to him.

Brad was quietly thoughtful until they had cleaned up and stacked the dishes. "Let's go into the library and talk this out," he suggested, draping his arm around her shoulders.

He was being very good-natured about this, but she wondered if he might be thinking why he ever got himself involved with two sisters who could *not* seem to keep their affairs private. Whatever he thought, she was gratified when he summarized the dilemma for her more simply than she would have thought possible.

"Honey, let's figure out what the right thing to do would be if Helena's telling the truth," he said. "She'd have to disclose her contacts with Cullion, right?"

"I guess so."

"Okay. That would release him to corroborate the story. And you'd have to disclose the blackmail letter and tell how you delivered the money. Then the police would ask Cullion about the note you included and whether he got rid of it."

"I follow so far, Brad."

" If that's what happened, his story about protecting a third party and his claim of self-defense would become more credible. And maybe the charges against him would be reduced to manslaughter."

"I think I see that," she said. "On the other hand, what if Helena was looking to harm the blackmailer?"

"I can't see how she would ever admit that."

"How am I going to find out?"

"Well, you could put it to her with the best face on it – tell her you believe what she said – and tell her you both have to go to the police. What she says at that point will reveal a lot."

"She'll say that exposes her to the accessory charge."

"Yes, but since she claims it isn't true, she has to do the right thing. Nobody should go to jail for second-degree murder because telling the truth would be inconvenient for someone else."

~ ~ ~

The thought that a man was willing to incur a second-degree murder conviction rather than expose Angela to some ugly publicity determined her to seek the truth. In doing so, she hadn't forgotten the ties Cullion had to her first husband. Before this, she had thought of him as "that terrible little man." But the little man had sought redemption in prison and was trying to work out his salvation in a cheesy little storefront church. She had the sense now that he wasn't such a little man after all.

It was eight o'clock when Angela knocked softly on Helena's door. Brad had suggested putting it off until tomorrow; but if she did, she knew she wouldn't sleep tonight. He stood by her, holding her hand and waiting for Helena to answer.

"Come in!" she called.

"Brad's with me, Helena. I hope we're not disturbing you," Angela said as they walked into the suite.

Helena was sitting in the motorized scooter and aiming her remote at the television in the armoire.

"There. That's off. I was watching that awful local show, the one that shows all sleaze, all the time."

"You mean FriscoTales?" Brad asked. "Our very own biography channel?"

"Oh Brad, that's clever. Yes, that's the one. Whenever I

forget my name is 'Helena Swann, the Black Widow,' I turn it on to remind myself."

Angela laughed. "I swear people who haven't met me think I have three last names," she said. "I'm always Angela Styles-Prominent-Socialite."

Helena moved towards the grouping of chairs in the middle of the suite. She never received guests while sitting in the scooter, so she shifted herself into an armchair and waited for Brad and Angela to get settled on the couch.

"I'd love to think we're just going to get cozy and chat," she said. "But somehow ..."

Brad interrupted.

"Hilary Saunders asked to meet with us this morning, Helena."

"Ah. I can't tell you how long it's been since I've seen Hilary."

"The Chief of Police and Lieutenant Bowers were there as well."

"How very ominous. What did they want?"

"It was about your telephone call mostly. They want us to ask you about it. That part wasn't a surprise."

"There's something else, isn't there?"

"Yes, something very unexpected happened. We could tell Hilary was surprised too. Lieutenant Bowers came clean about helping you locate Mickey Cullion just before Snider was murdered. And he wants us to think about why Cullion had ten thousand dollars in his room."

"I see. What did you say?"

Brad shrugged.

"We're thinking about it, as he requested."

"Well, that's your business, of course. Just don't expect me to talk to any of them about the phone call."

"Helena," Angela said, "as soon as Cullion's lawyer knows about the call, it will be in the press. They'll hound us day and night about it."

"Let them! I don't care! What good will it do to talk about it?"

Brad spoke up again.

"It could be the difference between murder and manslaughter to Mickey Cullion. Angela will have to tell them about the blackmail letter and the money as well. I'm positive Cullion has been covering up for both of you."

"In what way is he covering up for me? I only called him to find out who was blackmailing Angela."

"We're afraid the defense could claim you ... promised him something if he got rid of Jake Snider."

"You mean that's what *you two* think! Accessory to murder?"

"Helena, please!" Brad begged. "We're not accusing you of anything. We just want to do what's right."

"What's right for Mickey Cullion, you mean. And why are you so focused on him? Think of the awful publicity for Angela. And think of me! That letter claims I was an accessory to murder eight years ago. That makes twice! I might as well declare it my occupation!"

"But you know it isn't true, Helena."

Angela felt very uncomfortable and Brad's face was ashen.

"Isn't my existence miserable enough?" Helena asked. "Why can't you leave well enough alone? If you want to get rid of me, just tell me to go. But don't send me to Chowchilla so Cullion can serve two years instead of ten. Just kick me out and be done with it!"

"That about does it for me," Brad said, rising from the couch.

"Sure Brad, go. Just as you did the last time I really needed you."

"Helena, don't," Angela said. "This is too embarrassing. You've no right!"

"Oh, haven't I?"

Brad had drawn himself up to his full height and Angela could see he was trying hard to control himself.

"Yes, we had a relationship once and I ended it," he said. "I ended it when you nearly destroyed me. Angela won't admit it, but you nearly destroyed her as well. Do you honestly find it exceptional that we took solace in each other after that ... catastrophe?"

Helena turned her head aside in anger, hands trembling in her lap. In a teary blur, Angela saw Brad stride out of the room. She wiped her eyes, then rushed out to follow him. But he hadn't waited for her.

CHAPTER 16

Even though he was a powerful executive in a large organization, Brad Styles was able to maintain his reputation as a nice guy. He was bred to values like politeness and consideration, and it showed. Over the years, many people had peeked behind the scenes at Sharples to find out who *really* ran things – the reporters and competitors who took Brad's measure just couldn't reconcile the fellow they met with the success of his organization.

Brad wouldn't even assume the high-falutin' titles of his colleagues in the industry. He remained satisfied with his fifteen-year-old job description as Executive Director. In the company organization chart, he reported to his wife Angela, who was president. Her title was mainly a fiction, but Brad insisted she keep it. The reasons were partly sentimental – her father Sam Sharples founded the company – and partly pragmatic, because her name and heritage carried a long way in the business and social worlds of San Francisco.

As nice a guy as Brad Styles was, however, he could be pushed too far. And Helena had pushed especially hard the night he and Angela tried to convince her to reveal her contact with Mickey Cullion. After the emotional scene in Helena's suite, he stormed out into the corridor. When Helena followed a few moments later, he had already disappeared. Brad knew Angela would begin her search for him downstairs. When he was looking for privacy, he would usually retreat there to the library.

But not this time. He heard his wife call out while he paced their bedroom. She would find him soon enough, he thought. Rather than answer, he would attempt to be quiet and calm down. He pulled off his shoes, polo shirt and Dockers and looked into his massive chest of drawers for something comfortable. Finding a black tee and tan shorts, he put them on and padded barefoot over to the right of the French doors that gave out onto the balcony above the garden. There he opened the oak armoire that housed a mini-office he used only occasionally. He flipped open the laptop and booted up. While waiting, he took deep breaths: four counts inhale, four counts hold, four counts exhale.

Brad had logged on and accessed the Internet by the time Angela walked into the room.

"Well, there you are," she said. "I thought you had taken a walk when I couldn't find you downstairs."

"I heard you call me, but I had to cool off before I spoke again. I would have started yelling and God knows what would have come out. Helena has an extraordinary capacity for evil at times. Right now I feel outright hatred for her."

"Oh, Brad, that's so hard."

"Yes, it is. But it's true, Angela. I felt my heart harden towards her. I hate to lay down ultimatums, dear, but she can no longer live in this house."

"This is her home, Brad. Please don't ..."

"It's either hers or mine, it can't be both any longer."

"But she's my sister, Brad."

"Yes. She always will be. I wouldn't try to keep you from seeing her, Angela. I just don't want her around me anymore. And I'd prefer it if Justin only saw her in your company."

"Brad, please give her time. I think she'll finally do the right thing."

"She may, I suppose. And you may be surprised to know I believe her now. But it doesn't alter my conviction that she'd rather see a man sent up for murder than inconvenience her precious ass. It doesn't lessen the bitterness in her heart over every perceived injustice the world has inflicted on her. And it won't change the way I feel. I've had enough of Helena Swann for a lifetime."

"I believe her too, and yet I know you're right. I never thought it would come to this ... but I'll do it ... I'll tell her soon."

Brad had come over to where Angela sat on the bed. He drew her close and buried his face in the long, blond hair.

~ ~ ~

Overnight, Angela had grown used to the idea that Helena needed to establish her own life apart from them. It bothered her to think she was throwing a disabled woman out of the home she had known for nearly ten years, but she would help her in every way she could. What she couldn't reconcile herself to was making the further demand that Helena speak to the police about contacting Cullion and meeting with him.

Perhaps I could take that on myself, she thought. She was already prepared to give them the blackmail letter and relate what subsequently happened. Why not admit to a telephone call and a meeting with Cullion, just as if they had been her actions instead of Helena's? It seemed to make perfect sense. And yet she realized that the letter's charge of culpability in the murder of Wanda Buckley still accrued to Helena. She couldn't change that.

How could she go back to her on this point? That thought was much on her mind the following morning. Helena hadn't come down for breakfast, and she supposed she wouldn't see her all day unless she made it a point to invade her suite.

When Brad strolled into the kitchen for coffee, she told him her plan.

"Honey, you are so courageous!" he said. "But I don't

see how it could work. You were busy that Saturday – people could be found to testify you were elsewhere. And Cullion could burst your bubble at any moment by saying it's not true."

"I hadn't thought of that. I suppose you're right."

"You know, yesterday you said that Helena would do the right thing eventually. We're not so pressed for time that we can't wait a little for that to happen."

"But she can be awfully stubborn. After last night, she won't think about doing the right thing for days and days."

Brad laughed.

"Yes, I think I made sure of that." he said. "Tell you what. Now that I've cooled off, I believe Helena and I need to have a long chat. She won't be expecting that, so it just might be the right idea at the right time."

"What could you possibly have left to say to each other?"

"Lots of things, really. We can clear the air and go from there."

"Brad, you amaze me."

"Bullshit, Angela. I amaze no one."

"You're not going to tell her to leave, are you? Not today?"

"That's a thought. Who knows?"

~ ~ ~

Brad kept turning over in his mind what he would say to Helena and how she might reply. In the end, it didn't help him very much to go through all that, he thought. They had accumulated so much baggage during the past twenty years he was at a loss to predict how they would interact. It might go very nicely, or it could be a disaster. With Helena who could tell?

They had been lovers during college. Years later, when she returned from New York, she married Jeremy Swann. Brad's first marriage was on the rocks at that time. Five years later, they were both divorced and lonely. In all that time, she was never far from his mind.

He was already in charge of the Sharples empire. Naturally, he saw both sisters often; in fact, he was practically one of the family. Oh, how he had loved her! Steady, studious, reliable Brad in love with the dark-haired belle of every ball she attended. She was witty and poised and even a little dangerous. When they became engaged, he was the happiest man he knew.

The ugly saga of Porkpie put an end to his illusions and his happiness. Every aspect of their lives was subject to exploitation for months. He still regarded reporters as piranha or worse. When everything settled down, he had grown very close to Angela. Helena's eventual return to San Francisco generated no alarm and very little emotion for him. When he saw he had to help integrate her into his new life with Angela, he accepted the burden willingly. He did it because his wife's magnanimity and forgiveness was an unparalleled example of goodness to him.

Night was falling as he ascended the staircase to the second floor and walked quietly along the corridor to Helena's suite. He knocked three times and waited. She called for him to come in.

She was in the motorized chair looking out the large windows over the circular drive. Her back was to him as he walked in. How well he remembered the long, wavy hair, still as dark and glossy today as ever. He stopped a few steps into the room and waited. He was smiling at her as she turned to greet her visitor.

"Brad ... I never expected to see you today."

"I guess I'm surprised myself. But when you think and think and you can't get things out of your mind, it's best to turn to someone who knows you well."

"Do we know each other well, Brad? I'm not sure I feel that way any longer. Although I certainly did once."

"I think we do. I know we remind each other of some very unpleasant facts of life, but can you name a single person in San Francisco who is better qualified to write your biography than I am?"

Helena smiled and nodded.

"That's so," she said. "But don't you dare! And I'll promise not to write yours."

"Such a dull affair by comparison!" he answered.

"Not dull, no. You would look far too trusting and ... easy at times perhaps, but ultimately heroic. Whereas I ... I would be glamorous and evil by turns, and ultimately pathetic."

"Pathetic? How I disagree. And evil? You must be feeling a bit sorry for yourself tonight."

"Yes. I guess I am. Brad, I'm glad you came to see me. Tell me what it is you want to say."

"What I hope to get across is that we're going to get through this, Helena. You and Angela are going to get through it and so am I. We've had more difficult things to handle and we managed. We don't have to be afraid if we do it together."

Helena's right hand went to her platinum neck chain as she looked Brad full in the face.

"You're right. And it's the same thing you said yesterday, but everything got in the way. My strength is brittle, Brad; I can't always make a right decision, but I can sure stand on my rights until the cows come home. When you came in here with Angela last night, I suddenly wanted to hurt both of you. Whatever was right for you couldn't be right for me. You know? Sometimes I feel like a bitter old woman!"

"Don't, Helena. There's no need. I'm even glad you balked last night. I think I've found a way out that works for both of us. We just have to ... get rid of something."

He could see her face change from doubt and sadness to conspiratorial anticipation and outright glee. What an incredible creature she is, he thought.

CHAPTER 17

Shonda Wallace was Cullion's public defender. She was a big black gal with her hair in cornrows and heavy gold hoops in her ears. Cullion liked her – she was aggressive and smart. They joked with each other about their odd couple appearance: the little white dude with the enormous black female defender.

"You know, Michael," she deadpanned, "when I get you off, I'm gonna dress you up and you can be my pimp."

"Sounds cool," he said. "I could take the tricks you don't like and do them for you."

But his prospects were grim, and the light moments between them were few. Nearly every day, she asked him to go over his story. Why wouldn't he talk about the third party he was trying to protect? Where did Jake get ten thousand dollars? Was he *sure* the fight wasn't about the money or some other guy?

Hell, she had to know he didn't *want* to be charged with second-degree murder. "Won't the jury believe that I acted in self-defense?" he asked.

"Maybe and maybe not," she said. "Michael, when a guy slugs you and you rip his guts out, a jury is inclined to think you're worse than he is."

She tried hard to convince him to give her the name of the person he was trying to shield. His best bet was a plea bargain, which was impossible without a name, somebody to corroborate his story.

"Is it that Julie Reyes who comes to see you?" she asked.

"No," he said, "not Julie."

Today was different, though. Shonda wasn't full of questions. When she sat down with him, he could tell she was bothered about something.

"We're going to a meeting today, Michael."

"Both of us?"

"Yeah, you too. No leg chains, but you'll be cuffed in front. I've got your clothes, so you won't have to go in the jumpsuit."

"So? What's it all about?"

"Michael, I wish I could tell you. I threw one big ass fit, but it didn't help. All they would say is that it could be to your advantage."

"Sounds good, no? Who is 'they' anyway?"

"'They' is a hell of a lineup. The president of the Police Commission, the chief of police, and the D.A."

"Heavy, Shonda."

"Heavy, yes. So I wish your story wasn't such a lightweight, know what I'm sayin'?"

"It is what it is, Shonda. I can't help it."

"Oh yes you can, dammit!" she said. "I know you can!"

~ ~ ~

Around two o'clock Shonda and Cullion were escorted into a conference room at 850 Bryant Street. The sheriff guarding him was asked to wait outside. The lady who identified herself as president of the Police Commission introduced the police chief and the D.A. Cullion didn't catch anybody's name; he was self-conscious about the handcuffs and tried to keep his arms off the table.

He remembered Shonda saying the commissioner was Ms. Saunders, a well-known liberal activist she admired. Well, this lady was saying something about private citizens volunteering information – and all of a sudden the conference room door opened again. Shonda tensed up and put her hand on his forearm as Angela Styles walked into the room followed by Brad Styles wheeling Helena Swann. Oh man, what way was this gonna go?

Ms. Saunders was speaking again. "Mr. Cullion, I

understand you know Mr. and Mrs. Styles and Mrs. Swann."

"Yes I do," he said. Out of the corner of his eye, he could see Shonda turn to him with her mouth open and her eyes bugged out.

It was hard to watch Angela Styles speak about what happened at the charity ball and the next day when she made the payoff to Jake. The poor woman's voice shook so bad he had to look away. He guessed that Brad Styles was there to help his wife get through it all. When her turn came, Helena looked straight at him as she told about their meeting. He got the feeling she was daring him to contradict her. But that wasn't necessary; she told it pretty straight.

The District Attorney asked Cullion if he had anything to add. Before he could reply, Shonda cut in.

"Excuse me, please. I'll see if my client has anything to say in just a moment. Right now we'd like to see the blackmail note Mrs. Styles mentioned."

"Mrs. Styles informs us she destroyed the letter." It was Ms. Saunders speaking. Cullion saw the D.A. nodding in agreement.

"I see," said Shonda. "But the copy? Mrs. Swann said she made a copy to show my client when they met."

Helena spoke up. "When my sister told me she destroyed the original, I disposed of the copy also. We were afraid it would be published eventually if we turned it over."

"And what about the note Mrs. Styles included with the money?"

The D.A. cleared his throat to speak. "It was never recovered," he said. "We don't know what happened to it."

Shonda's hands flew up. "There's no proof, so we just take their word for all this? How convenient!"

"Does your client dispute any of this, Ms. Wallace?"

Shonda leaned in and whispered to him.

"This is bullshit, Michael. Don't say anything for now. We're already down to manslaughter, and you may not even do time. Tell me what was in the blackmail letter. They're covering something up."

She had that nailed down. The sisters got rid of the blackmail letter because it pointed to Helena as an accessory to murder. If he shut up and talked it over with Shonda, he'd be in the driver's seat. His conscience told him that backing up Angela Styles with that story about her note to Jake was the right thing to do. Still, if the tables were turned, what would any of these people do for *him?*

Cullion exhaled and shook his head. "Thanks, Shonda. It's okay," he said. "There's something I need to say for Mrs. Styles here."

"No, Michael, don't!" she whispered furiously. "It's in your best interest to hold back. Say nothing!"

He looked her in the eye a moment while he fussed with his handcuffs. Her passion for his cause made him waver. Then he cleared his throat and looked out to the expectant faces around the table.

"Yeah, I got something I wanna say. When it was all over and Jake was dead, I started to think about the note Mrs. Styles put in with the money. Jake was real mad when he read it, so I went and got it out of the bag to figure out why. It didn't say much except she'd never give him more money, but she *signed* it, you know? I knew that would put her in the newspapers for sure. So I folded it small and shoved it down the slot for razor blades in back of the medicine cabinet. Then I went through Jake's pockets, got his keys and locked the duffel bag. Before the cops got there, I put the keys back."

Like a gush of air let out of an overfilled balloon, the tension in the room dissipated as Cullion spoke. If Shonda was uptight still, everyone else had relaxed. The D.A. turned off the recorder and stepped outside to signal the sheriff. Cullion and Shonda were escorted out of the building.

CHAPTER 18

When Dan Cinzano got back from the big meeting, Al Bowers was waiting for him. He had a feeling his career was on the line, and he had to be the first to know. If necessary, he was prepared to resign. Cinzano lumbered into his office and flopped in his chair. Bowers couldn't read his expression. His boss looked straight at him, nodded, then yanked his tie off.

"C'mon Chief, talk!" Bowers said.

"It's all politics, Al, you know that? Politics ... advantage ... and power."

"Please, Dan ...."

The Chief was smiling, toying with him. He settled in at his desk, cleared his throat, and explained how Angela Styles and Helena Swann figured into the case with Cullion. Then he looked up at Bowers and grimaced, as if he were still puzzled about something.

"Lessee now ... after the meeting, Brad Styles cornered me, the D.A., and Hilary. Styles had a 'concern' about any further press coverage. He announced Mrs. Styles wants to donate the recovered ten grand, which he'll match, to the Police Athletic League or other charity we choose – *as soon as the case is closed.* 'No Publicity' writ large ... is what I got out of it. The D. A. and Hilary will hafta try to rein in Shonda Wallace. Styles never said so, but there'll be no check for twenty grand if his wife and sister-in-law come to grief in the press."

"What'll happen to Cullion, Chief?"

"The D. A. will reduce the charge. With his priors, though, he'll do some time. Maybe a year."

Bowers was shaking his head. "So ... no publicity for Angela Styles or Helena Swann, no public spanking for me, and no second-degree murder charge for Mickey Cullion. Man, what's it all about, Chief? What was it Jake Snider put in the blackmail letter that made it turn out this way?"

"That's what everybody wants to know. No doubt he had something on one of our socialite buddies."

It seemed to Bowers that Brad Styles must be some kind of genius for engineering the whole wrap-up. In the end, the folks with the most to lose had made it to port safely. The ones who wouldn't get their payoff would be the media and the part of the public that salivates over scandal. He began to laugh, quietly at first, then louder until Cinzano pushed away from his desk and glared at him.

"You can laugh, Al, but it's Hilary Saunders who winds up in the catbird seat. That bitch put me on notice the twenty grand will go to *her* favorite charities, while I have to be content that my Homicide Detail isn't dragged through the mud for compromising the case. 'Screw the Police Athletic League' were her exact words, I believe."

Bowers make a coughing sound to cut the laughter short. He realized he owed his boss big time for that.

Thank you for reading.
Please review this book. Reviews help others find New Pulp Press and inspire us to keep providing these marvelous tales.

If you would like to be put on our email list to receive updates on new releases, contests, and promotions, please go to NewPulpPress.com and sign up.

ABOUT THE AUTHOR

Paul McGoran lives in Newport, Rhode Island. In his life before fiction, he was a laboratory technician, a Russian language interpreter for the U. S. Navy, a career marketing executive, a management consultant, and a day trader. As a writer in the crime genre since 2005, his inspiration comes in equal parts from spending way too much time watching black and white film noir from the forties and fifties, and from reading way too many hard-boiled detective stories.

Paul's first novel, *Made for Murder*, is available in paperback and eBook versions. Watch for his second novel from New Pulp Press, *The Breastplate of Faith and Love*, which will introduce a series P.I. named Stafford Boyle. Paul is currently working on a second novel, *Sooner or Later, Delicate Death,* which takes Staff Boyle back to his old hometown to solve the revenge murder of the neighborhood bully who terrorized his childhood.

NewPulpPress.com